The Door in the Wall, and Other Stories

by

H. G. (Herbert George) Wells

TABLE OF CONTENTS

THE DOOR IN THE WALL.

I

One confidential evening, not three months ago, Lionel Wallace told me this story of the Door in the Wall. And at the time I thought that so far as he was concerned it was a true story.

He told it me with such a direct simplicity of conviction that I could not do otherwise than believe in him. But in the morning, in my own flat, I woke to a different atmosphere, and as I lay in bed and recalled the things he had told me, stripped of the glamour of his earnest slow voice, denuded of the focussed shaded table light, the shadowy atmosphere that wrapped about him and the pleasant bright things, the dessert and glasses and napery of the dinner we had shared, making them for the time a bright little world quite cut off from every-day realities, I saw it all as frankly incredible. "He was mystifying!" I said, and then: "How well he did it!. . . . . It isn't quite the thing I should have expected him, of all people, to do well."

Afterwards, as I sat up in bed and sipped my morning tea, I found myself trying to account for the flavour of reality that perplexed me in his impossible reminiscences, by supposing they did in some way suggest, present, convey--I hardly know which word to use--experiences it was otherwise impossible to tell.

Well, I don't resort to that explanation now. I have got over my intervening doubts. I believe now, as I believed at the moment of telling, that Wallace did to the very best of his ability strip the truth of his secret for me. But whether he himself saw, or only thought he saw, whether he himself was the possessor of an inestimable privilege, or the victim of a fantastic dream, I cannot pretend to guess. Even the facts of his death, which ended my doubts forever, throw no light on that. That much the reader must judge for himself.

I forget now what chance comment or criticism of mine moved so reticent a man to confide in me. He was, I think, defending himself against an imputation of slackness and unreliability I had made in relation to a great public movement in which he had disappointed me. But he plunged suddenly. "I have" he said, "a preoccupation--"

"I know," he went on, after a pause that he devoted to the study of his cigar ash, "I have been negligent. The fact is--it isn't a case of ghosts or apparitions--but--it's an odd thing to tell of, Redmond--I am haunted. I am haunted by something--that rather takes the light out of things, that fills me with longings . . . . ."

He paused, checked by that English shyness that so often overcomes us when we would speak of moving or grave or beautiful things. "You were at Saint Athelstan's all through," he said, and for a moment that seemed to me quite irrelevant. "Well"--and he paused. Then very haltingly at first, but afterwards more easily, he began to tell of the thing that was hidden in his life, the haunting memory of a beauty and a happiness that filled his heart with insatiable longings that made all the interests and spectacle of worldly life seem dull and tedious and vain to him.

Now that I have the clue to it, the thing seems written visibly in his face. I have a photograph in which that look of detachment has been caught and intensified. It reminds me of what a woman once said of him--a woman who had loved him greatly. "Suddenly," she said, "the interest goes out of him. He forgets you. He doesn't care a rap for you--under his very nose . . . . ."

Yet the interest was not always out of him, and when he was holding his attention to a thing Wallace could contrive to be an extremely successful man. His career, indeed, is set with successes. He left me behind him long ago; he soared up over my head, and cut a figure in the world that I couldn't cut--anyhow. He was still a year short of forty, and they say now that he would have been in office and very probably in the new Cabinet if he had lived. At school he always beat me without effort--as it were by nature. We were at school together at Saint Athelstan's College in West Kensington for almost all our school time. He came into the school as my co-equal, but he left far above me, in a blaze of scholarships and brilliant performance. Yet I think I made a fair average running. And it was at school I heard first of the Door in the Wall--that I was to hear of a second time only a month before his death.

To him at least the Door in the Wall was a real door leading through a real wall to immortal realities. Of that I am now quite assured.

And it came into his life early, when he was a little fellow between five and six. I remember how, as he sat making his confession to me with a slow gravity, he reasoned and reckoned the date of it. "There was," he said, "a crimson Virginia creeper in it--all one bright uniform crimson in a clear amber sunshine against a white wall. That came into the impression somehow, though I don't clearly remember how, and there were horse-chestnut leaves upon the clean pavement outside the green door. They were blotched yellow and green, you know, not brown nor dirty, so that they must have been new fallen. I take it that means October. I look out for horse-chestnut leaves every year, and I ought to know.

"If I'm right in that, I was about five years and four months old."

He was, he said, rather a precocious little boy--he learned to talk at an abnormally early age, and he was so sane and "old-fashioned," as people say, that he was permitted an amount of initiative that most children scarcely attain by seven or eight. His mother died when he was born, and he was under the less vigilant and authoritative care of a nursery governess. His father was a stern, preoccupied lawyer, who gave him little attention, and expected great things of him. For all his brightness he found life a little grey and dull I think. And one day he wandered.

He could not recall the particular neglect that enabled him to get away, nor the course he took among the West Kensington roads. All that had faded among the incurable blurs of memory. But the white wall and the green door stood out quite distinctly.

As his memory of that remote childish experience ran, he did at the very first sight of that door experience a peculiar emotion, an attraction, a desire to get to the door and open it and walk in.

And at the same time he had the clearest conviction that either it was unwise or it was wrong of him--he could not tell which--to yield to this attraction. He insisted upon it as a curious thing that he knew from the very beginning--unless memory has played him the queerest trick--that the door was unfastened, and that he could go in as he chose.

I seem to see the figure of that little boy, drawn and repelled. And it was very clear in his mind, too, though why it should be so was never explained, that his father would be very angry if he went through that door.

Wallace described all these moments of hesitation to me with the utmost particularity. He went right past the door, and then, with his hands in his pockets, and making an infantile attempt to whistle, strolled right along beyond the end of the wall. There he recalls a number of mean, dirty shops, and particularly that of a plumber and decorator, with a dusty disorder of earthenware pipes, sheet lead ball taps, pattern books of wall paper, and tins of enamel. He stood pretending to examine these things, and coveting, passionately desiring the green door.

Then, he said, he had a gust of emotion. He made a run for it, lest hesitation should grip him again, he went plump with outstretched hand through the green door and let it slam behind him. And so, in a trice, he came into the garden that has haunted all his life.

It was very difficult for Wallace to give me his full sense of that garden into which he came.

There was something in the very air of it that exhilarated, that gave one a sense of lightness and good happening and well being; there was something in the sight of it that made all its colour clean and perfect and subtly luminous. In the instant of coming into it one was exquisitely glad--as only in rare moments and when one is young and joyful one can be glad in this world. And everything was beautiful there . . . . .

Wallace mused before he went on telling me. "You see," he said, with the doubtful inflection of a man who pauses at incredible things, "there were two great panthers there . . . Yes, spotted panthers. And I was not afraid. There was a long wide path with marble-edged flower borders on either side, and these two huge velvety beasts were playing there with a ball. One looked up and came towards me, a little curious as it seemed. It came right up to me, rubbed its soft round ear very gently against the small hand I held out and purred. It was, I tell you, an enchanted garden. I know. And the size? Oh! it stretched far and wide, this way and that. I believe there were hills far away. Heaven knows where West Kensington had suddenly got to. And somehow it was just like coming home.

"You know, in the very moment the door swung to behind me, I forgot the road with its fallen chestnut leaves, its cabs and tradesmen's carts, I forgot the sort of gravitational pull back to the discipline and obedience of home, I forgot all hesitations and fear, forgot discretion, forgot all the intimate realities of this life. I became in a moment a very glad and wonder-happy little boy--in another world. It was a world with a different quality, a warmer, more penetrating and mellower light, with a faint clear gladness in its air, and wisps of sun-touched cloud in the blueness of its sky. And before me ran this long wide path, invitingly, with weedless beds on either side, rich with untended flowers, and these two great panthers. I put my little hands fearlessly on their soft fur, and caressed their round ears and the sensitive corners under their ears, and played with them, and it was as though they welcomed me home. There was a keen sense of home-coming in my mind, and when presently a tall, fair girl appeared in the pathway and came to meet me, smiling, and said 'Well?' to me, and lifted me, and kissed me, and put me down, and led me by the hand, there was no amazement, but only an impression of delightful rightness, of being reminded of happy things that had in some strange way been overlooked. There were broad steps, I remember, that came into view between spikes of delphinium, and up these we went to a great avenue between very old and shady dark trees. All down this avenue, you know, between the red chapped stems, were marble seats of honour and statuary, and very tame and friendly white doves . . . . .

"And along this avenue my girl-friend led me, looking down--I recall the pleasant lines, the finely-modelled chin of her sweet kind face--asking me questions in a soft, agreeable voice, and telling me things, pleasant things I know, though what they were I was never able to recall . . . And presently a little Capuchin monkey, very clean, with a fur of ruddy brown and kindly hazel eyes, came down a tree to us and ran beside me, looking up at me and grinning, and presently leapt to my shoulder. So we went on our way in great happiness . . . ."

He paused.

"Go on," I said.

"I remember little things. We passed an old man musing among laurels, I remember, and a place gay with paroquets, and came through a broad shaded colonnade to a spacious cool palace, full of pleasant fountains, full of beautiful things, full of the quality and promise of heart's desire. And there were many things and many people, some that still seem to stand out clearly and some that are a little vague, but all these people were beautiful and kind. In some way--I don't know how--it was conveyed to me that they all were kind to me, glad to have me there, and filling me with gladness by their gestures, by the touch of their hands, by the welcome and love in their eyes. Yes--"

He mused for awhile. "Playmates I found there. That was very much to me, because I was a lonely little boy. They played delightful games in a grass-covered court where there was a sun-dial set about with flowers. And as one played one loved . . . .

"But--it's odd--there's a gap in my memory. I don't remember the games we played. I never remembered. Afterwards, as a child, I spent long hours trying, even with tears, to recall the form of that happiness. I wanted to play it all over again--in my nursery --by myself. No! All I remember is the happiness and two dear playfellows who were most with me . . . . Then presently came a sombre dark woman, with a grave, pale face and dreamy eyes, a sombre woman wearing a soft long robe of pale purple, who carried a book and beckoned and took me aside with her into a gallery above a hall--though my playmates were loth to have me go, and ceased their game and stood watching as I was carried away. 'Come back to us!' they cried. 'Come back to us soon!' I looked up at her face, but she heeded them not at all. Her face was very gentle and grave. She took me to a seat in the gallery, and I stood beside her, ready to look at her book as she opened it upon her knee. The pages fell open. She pointed, and I looked, marvelling, for in the living pages of that book I saw myself; it was a story about myself, and in it were all the things that had happened to me since ever I was born . . . .

"It was wonderful to me, because the pages of that book were not pictures, you understand, but realities."

Wallace paused gravely--looked at me doubtfully.

"Go on," I said. "I understand."

"They were realities--yes, they must have been; people moved and things came and went in them; my dear mother, whom I had near forgotten; then my father, stern and upright, the servants, the nursery, all the familiar things of home. Then the front door and the busy streets, with traffic to and fro: I looked and marvelled, and looked half doubtfully again into the woman's face and turned the pages over, skipping this and that, to see more of this book, and more, and so at last I came to myself hovering and hesitating outside the green door in the long white wall, and felt again the conflict and the fear.

"'And next?' I cried, and would have turned on, but the cool hand of the grave woman delayed me.

"'Next?' I insisted, and struggled gently with her hand, pulling up her fingers with all my childish strength, and as she yielded and the page came over she bent down upon me like a shadow and kissed my brow.

"But the page did not show the enchanted garden, nor the panthers, nor the girl who had led me by the hand, nor the playfellows who had been so loth to let me go. It showed a long grey street in West Kensington, on that chill hour of afternoon before the lamps are lit, and I was there, a wretched little figure, weeping aloud, for all that I could do to restrain myself, and I was weeping because I could not return to my dear play-fellows who had called after me, 'Come back to us! Come back to us soon!' I was there. This was no page in a book, but harsh reality; that enchanted place and the restraining hand of the grave mother at whose knee I stood had gone--whither have they gone?"

He halted again, and remained for a time, staring into the fire.

"Oh! the wretchedness of that return!" he murmured.

"Well?" I said after a minute or so.

"Poor little wretch I was--brought back to this grey world again! As I realised the fulness of what had happened to me, I gave way to quite ungovernable grief. And the shame and humiliation of that public weeping and my disgraceful homecoming remain with me still. I see again the benevolent-looking old gentleman in gold spectacles who stopped and spoke to me--prodding me first with his umbrella. 'Poor little chap,' said he; 'and are you lost then?'--and me a London boy of five and more! And he must needs bring in a kindly young policeman and make a crowd of me, and so march me home. Sobbing, conspicuous and frightened, I came from the enchanted garden to the steps of my father's house.

"That is as well as I can remember my vision of that garden--the garden that haunts me still. Of course, I can convey nothing of that indescribable quality of translucent unreality, that difference from the common things of experience that hung about it all; but that--that is what happened. If it was a dream, I am sure it was a day-time and altogether extraordinary dream . . . . . . H'm!--naturally there followed a terrible questioning, by my aunt, my father, the nurse, the governess--everyone . . . . . .

"I tried to tell them, and my father gave me my first thrashing for telling lies. When afterwards I tried to tell my aunt, she punished me again for my wicked persistence. Then, as I said, everyone was forbidden to listen to me, to hear a word about it. Even my fairy tale books were taken away from me for a time--because I was 'too imaginative.' Eh? Yes, they did that! My father belonged to the old school . . . . . And my story was driven back upon myself. I whispered it to my pillow--my pillow that was often damp and salt to my whispering lips with childish tears. And I added always to my official and less fervent prayers this one heartfelt request: 'Please God I may dream of the garden. Oh! take me back to my garden! Take me back to my garden!'

"I dreamt often of the garden. I may have added to it, I may have changed it; I do not know . . . . . All this you understand is an attempt to reconstruct from fragmentary memories a very early experience. Between that and the other consecutive memories of my boyhood there is a gulf. A time came when it seemed impossible I should ever speak of that wonder glimpse again."

I asked an obvious question.

"No," he said. "I don't remember that I ever attempted to find my way back to the garden in those early years. This seems odd to me now, but I think that very probably a closer watch was kept on my movements after this misadventure to prevent my going astray. No, it wasn't until you knew me that I tried for the garden again. And I believe there was a period --incredible as it seems now--when I forgot the garden altogether--when I was about eight or nine it may have been. Do you remember me as a kid at Saint Athelstan's?"

"Rather!"

"I didn't show any signs did I in those days of having a secret dream?"

II

He looked up with a sudden smile.

"Did you ever play North-West Passage with me? . . . . . No, of course you didn't come my way!"

"It was the sort of game," he went on, "that every imaginative child plays all day. The idea was the discovery of a North-West Passage to school. The way to school was plain enough; the game consisted in finding some way that wasn't plain, starting off ten minutes early in some almost hopeless direction, and working one's way round through unaccustomed streets to my goal. And one day I got entangled among some rather low-class streets on the other side of Campden Hill, and I began to think that for once the game would be against me and that I should get to school late. I tried rather desperately a street that seemed a cul de sac, and found a passage at the end. I hurried through that with renewed hope. 'I shall do it yet,' I said, and passed a row of frowsy little shops that were inexplicably familiar to me, and behold! there was my long white wall and the green door that led to the enchanted garden!

"The thing whacked upon me suddenly. Then, after all, that garden, that wonderful garden, wasn't a dream!" . . . .

He paused.

"I suppose my second experience with the green door marks the world of difference there is between the busy life of a schoolboy and the infinite leisure of a child. Anyhow, this second time I didn't for a moment think of going in straight away. You see . . . For one thing my mind was full of the idea of getting to school in time--set on not breaking my record for punctuality. I must surely have felt SOME little desire at least to try the door--yes, I must have felt that . . . . . But I seem to remember the attraction of the door mainly as another obstacle to my overmastering determination to get to school. I was immediately interested by this discovery I had made, of course--I went on with my mind full of it--but I went on. It didn't check me. I ran past tugging out my watch, found I had ten minutes still to spare, and then I was going downhill into familiar surroundings. I got to school, breathless, it is true, and wet with perspiration, but in time. I can remember hanging up my coat and hat . . . Went right by it and left it behind me. Odd, eh?"

He looked at me thoughtfully. "Of course, I didn't know then that it wouldn't always be there. School boys have limited imaginations. I suppose I thought it was an awfully jolly thing to have it there, to know my way back to it, but there was the school tugging at me. I expect I was a good deal distraught and inattentive that morning, recalling what I could of the beautiful strange people I should presently see again. Oddly enough I had no doubt in my mind that they would be glad to see me . . . Yes, I must have thought of the garden that morning just as a jolly sort of place to which one might resort in the interludes of a strenuous scholastic career.

"I didn't go that day at all. The next day was a half holiday, and that may have weighed with me. Perhaps, too, my state of inattention brought down impositions upon me and docked the margin of time necessary for the detour. I don't know. What I do know is that in the meantime the enchanted garden was so much upon my mind that I could not keep it to myself.

"I told--What was his name?--a ferrety-looking youngster we used to call Squiff."

"Young Hopkins," said I.

"Hopkins it was. I did not like telling him, I had a feeling that in some way it was against the rules to tell him, but I did. He was walking part of the way home with me; he was talkative, and if we had not talked about the enchanted garden we should have talked of something else, and it was intolerable to me to think about any other subject. So I blabbed.

"Well, he told my secret. The next day in the play interval I found myself surrounded by half a dozen bigger boys, half teasing and wholly curious to hear more of the enchanted garden. There was that big Fawcett--you remember him?--and Carnaby and Morley Reynolds. You weren't there by any chance? No, I think I should have remembered if you were . . . . .

"A boy is a creature of odd feelings. I was, I really believe, in spite of my secret self-disgust, a little flattered to have the attention of these big fellows. I remember particularly a moment of pleasure caused by the praise of Crawshaw--you remember Crawshaw major, the son of Crawshaw the composer?--who said it was the best lie he had ever heard. But at the same time there was a really painful undertow of shame at telling what I felt was indeed a sacred secret. That beast Fawcett made a joke about the girl in green--."

Wallace's voice sank with the keen memory of that shame. "I pretended not to hear," he said. "Well, then Carnaby suddenly called me a young liar and disputed with me when I said the thing was true. I said I knew where to find the green door, could lead them all there in ten minutes. Carnaby became outrageously virtuous, and said I'd have to--and bear out my words or suffer. Did you ever have Carnaby twist your arm? Then perhaps you'll understand how it went with me. I swore my story was true. There was nobody in the school then to save a chap from Carnaby though Crawshaw put in a word or so. Carnaby had got his game. I grew excited and red-eared, and a little frightened, I behaved altogether like a silly little chap, and the outcome of it all was that instead of starting alone for my enchanted garden, I led the way presently--cheeks flushed, ears hot, eyes smarting, and my soul one burning misery and shame--for a party of six mocking, curious and threatening school-fellows.

"We never found the white wall and the green door . . ."

"You mean?--"

"I mean I couldn't find it. I would have found it if I could.

"And afterwards when I could go alone I couldn't find it. I never found it. I seem now to have been always looking for it through my school-boy days, but I've never come upon it again."

"Did the fellows--make it disagreeable?"

"Beastly . . . . . Carnaby held a council over me for wanton lying. I remember how I sneaked home and upstairs to hide the marks of my blubbering. But when I cried myself to sleep at last it wasn't for Carnaby, but for the garden, for the beautiful afternoon I had hoped for, for the sweet friendly women and the waiting playfellows and the game I had hoped to learn again, that beautiful forgotten game . . . . .

"I believed firmly that if I had not told-- . . . . . I had bad times after that--crying at night and woolgathering by day. For two terms I slackened and had bad reports. Do you remember? Of course you would! It was YOU--your beating me in mathematics that brought me back to the grind again."

III

For a time my friend stared silently into the red heart of the fire. Then he said: "I never saw it again until I was seventeen.

"It leapt upon me for the third time--as I was driving to Paddington on my way to Oxford and a scholarship. I had just one momentary glimpse. I was leaning over the apron of my hansom smoking a cigarette, and no doubt thinking myself no end of a man of the world, and suddenly there was the door, the wall, the dear sense of unforgettable and still attainable things.

"We clattered by--I too taken by surprise to stop my cab until we were well past and round a corner. Then I had a queer moment, a double and divergent movement of my will: I tapped the little door in the roof of the cab, and brought my arm down to pull out my watch. 'Yes, sir!' said the cabman, smartly. 'Er-- well--it's nothing,' I cried. 'MY mistake! We haven't much time! Go on!' and he went on . . .

"I got my scholarship. And the night after I was told of that I sat over my fire in my little upper room, my study, in my father's house, with his praise--his rare praise--and his sound counsels ringing in my ears, and I smoked my favourite pipe--the formidable bulldog of adolescence--and thought of that door in the long white wall. 'If I had stopped,' I thought, 'I should have missed my scholarship, I should have missed Oxford--muddled all the fine career before me! I begin to see things better!' I fell musing deeply, but I did not doubt then this career of mine was a thing that merited sacrifice.

"Those dear friends and that clear atmosphere seemed very sweet to me, very fine, but remote. My grip was fixing now upon the world. I saw another door opening--the door of my career."

He stared again into the fire. Its red lights picked out a stubborn strength in his face for just one flickering moment, and then it vanished again.

"Well", he said and sighed, "I have served that career. I have done--much work, much hard work. But I have dreamt of the enchanted garden a thousand dreams, and seen its door, or at least glimpsed its door, four times since then. Yes--four times. For a while this world was so bright and interesting, seemed so full of meaning and opportunity that the half-effaced charm of the garden was by comparison gentle and remote. Who wants to pat panthers on the way to dinner with pretty women and distinguished men? I came down to London from Oxford, a man of bold promise that I have done something to redeem. Something--and yet there have been disappointments . . . . .

"Twice I have been in love--I will not dwell on that--but once, as I went to someone who, I know, doubted whether I dared to come, I took a short cut at a venture through an unfrequented road near Earl's Court, and so happened on a white wall and a familiar green door. 'Odd!' said I to myself, 'but I thought this place was on Campden Hill. It's the place I never could find somehow--like counting Stonehenge--the place of that queer day dream of mine.' And I went by it intent upon my purpose. It had no appeal to me that afternoon.

"I had just a moment's impulse to try the door, three steps aside were needed at the most--though I was sure enough in my heart that it would open to me--and then I thought that doing so might delay me on the way to that appointment in which I thought my honour was involved. Afterwards I was sorry for my punctuality--I might at least have peeped in I thought, and waved a hand to those panthers, but I knew enough by this time not to seek again belatedly that which is not found by seeking. Yes, that time made me very sorry . . . . .

"Years of hard work after that and never a sight of the door. It's only recently it has come back to me. With it there has come a sense as though some thin tarnish had spread itself over my world. I began to think of it as a sorrowful and bitter thing that I should never see that door again. Perhaps I was suffering a little from overwork--perhaps it was what I've heard spoken of as the feeling of forty. I don't know. But certainly the keen brightness that makes effort easy has gone out of things recently, and that just at a time with all these new political developments --when I ought to be working. Odd, isn't it? But I do begin to find life toilsome, its rewards, as I come near them, cheap. I began a little while ago to want the garden quite badly. Yes--and I've seen it three times."

"The garden?"

"No--the door! And I haven't gone in!"

He leaned over the table to me, with an enormous sorrow in his voice as he spoke. "Thrice I have had my chance--THRICE! If ever that door offers itself to me again, I swore, I will go in out of this dust and heat, out of this dry glitter of vanity, out of these toilsome futilities. I will go and never return. This time I will stay . . . . . I swore it and when the time came-- I DIDN'T GO.

"Three times in one year have I passed that door and failed to enter. Three times in the last year.

"The first time was on the night of the snatch division on the Tenants' Redemption Bill, on which the Government was saved by a majority of three. You remember? No one on our side--perhaps very few on the opposite side--expected the end that night. Then the debate collapsed like eggshells. I and Hotchkiss were dining with his cousin at Brentford, we were both unpaired, and we were called up by telephone, and set off at once in his cousin's motor. We got in barely in time, and on the way we passed my wall and door--livid in the moonlight, blotched with hot yellow as the glare of our lamps lit it, but unmistakable. 'My God!' cried I. 'What?'said Hotchkiss. 'Nothing!' I answered, and the moment passed.

"'I've made a great sacrifice,' I told the whip as I got in. 'They all have,' he said, and hurried by.

"I do not see how I could have done otherwise then. And the next occasion was as I rushed to my father's bedside to bid that stern old man farewell. Then, too, the claims of life were imperative. But the third time was different; it happened a week ago. It fills me with hot remorse to recall it. I was with Gurker and Ralphs--it's no secret now you know that I've had my talk with Gurker. We had been dining at Frobisher's, and the talk had become intimate between us. The question of my place in the reconstructed ministry lay always just over the boundary of the discussion. Yes --yes. That's all settled. It needn't be talked about yet, but there's no reason to keep a secret from you . . . . . Yes--thanks! thanks! But let me tell you my story.

"Then, on that night things were very much in the air. My position was a very delicate one. I was keenly anxious to get some definite word from Gurker, but was hampered by Ralphs' presence. I was using the best power of my brain to keep that light and careless talk not too obviously directed to the point that concerns me. I had to. Ralphs' behaviour since has more than justified my caution . . . . . Ralphs, I knew, would leave us beyond the Kensington High Street, and then I could surprise Gurker by a sudden frankness. One has sometimes to resort to these little devices. . . . . And then it was that in the margin of my field of vision I became aware once more of the white wall, the green door before us down the road.

"We passed it talking. I passed it. I can still see the shadow of Gurker's marked profile, his opera hat tilted forward over his prominent nose, the many folds of his neck wrap going before my shadow and Ralphs' as we sauntered past.

"I passed within twenty inches of the door. 'If I say good-night to them, and go in,' I asked myself, 'what will happen?' And I was all a-tingle for that word with Gurker.

"I could not answer that question in the tangle of my other problems. 'They will think me mad,' I thought. 'And suppose I vanish now!--Amazing disappearance of a prominent politician!' That weighed with me. A thousand inconceivably petty worldlinesses weighed with me in that crisis."

Then he turned on me with a sorrowful smile, and, speaking slowly; "Here I am!" he said.

"Here I am!" he repeated, "and my chance has gone from me. Three times in one year the door has been offered me--the door that goes into peace, into delight, into a beauty beyond dreaming, a kindness no man on earth can know. And I have rejected it, Redmond, and it has gone--"

"How do you know?"

"I know. I know. I am left now to work it out, to stick to the tasks that held me so strongly when my moments came. You say, I have success--this vulgar, tawdry, irksome, envied thing. I have it." He had a walnut in his big hand. "If that was my success," he said, and crushed it, and held it out for me to see.

"Let me tell you something, Redmond. This loss is destroying me. For two months, for ten weeks nearly now, I have done no work at all, except the most necessary and urgent duties. My soul is full of inappeasable regrets. At nights--when it is less likely I shall be recognised--I go out. I wander. Yes. I wonder what people would think of that if they knew. A Cabinet Minister, the responsible head of that most vital of all departments, wandering alone--grieving--sometimes near audibly lamenting--for a door, for a garden!"

IV

I can see now his rather pallid face, and the unfamiliar sombre fire that had come into his eyes. I see him very vividly to-night. I sit recalling his words, his tones, and last evening's Westminster Gazette still lies on my sofa, containing the notice of his death. At lunch to-day the club was busy with him and the strange riddle of his fate.

They found his body very early yesterday morning in a deep excavation near East Kensington Station. It is one of two shafts that have been made in connection with an extension of the railway southward. It is protected from the intrusion of the public by a hoarding upon the high road, in which a small doorway has been cut for the convenience of some of the workmen who live in that direction. The doorway was left unfastened through a misunderstanding between two gangers, and through it he made his way . . . . .

My mind is darkened with questions and riddles.

It would seem he walked all the way from the House that night--he has frequently walked home during the past Session--and so it is I figure his dark form coming along the late and empty streets, wrapped up, intent. And then did the pale electric lights near the station cheat the rough planking into a semblance of white? Did that fatal unfastened door awaken some memory?

Was there, after all, ever any green door in the wall at all?

I do not know. I have told his story as he told it to me. There are times when I believe that Wallace was no more than the victim of the coincidence between a rare but not unprecedented type of hallucination and a careless trap, but that indeed is not my profoundest belief. You may think me superstitious if you will, and foolish; but, indeed, I am more than half convinced that he had in truth, an abnormal gift, and a sense, something--I know not what--that in the guise of wall and door offered him an outlet, a secret and peculiar passage of escape into another and altogether more beautiful world. At any rate, you will say, it betrayed him in the end. But did it betray him? There you touch the inmost mystery of these dreamers, these men of vision and the imagination.

We see our world fair and common, the hoarding and the pit. By our daylight standard he walked out of security into darkness, danger and death. But did he see like that?

THE STAR.

It was on the first day of the New Year that the announcement was made, almost simultaneously from three observatories, that the motion of the planet Neptune, the outermost of all the planets that wheel about the sun, had become very erratic. Ogilvy had already called attention to a suspected retardation in its velocity in December. Such a piece of news was scarcely calculated to interest a world the greater portion of whose inhabitants were unaware of the existence of the planet Neptune, nor outside the astronomical profession did the subsequent discovery of a faint remote speck of light in the region of the perturbed planet cause any very great excitement. Scientific people, however, found the intelligence remarkable enough, even before it became known that the new body was rapidly growing larger and brighter, that its motion was quite different from the orderly progress of the planets, and that the deflection of Neptune and its satellite was becoming now of an unprecedented kind.

Few people without a training in science can realise the huge isolation of the solar system. The sun with its specks of planets, its dust of planetoids, and its impalpable comets, swims in a vacant immensity that almost defeats the imagination. Beyond the orbit of Neptune there is space, vacant so far as human observation has penetrated, without warmth or light or sound, blank emptiness, for twenty million times a million miles. That is the smallest estimate of the distance to be traversed before the very nearest of the stars is attained. And, saving a few comets more unsubstantial than the thinnest flame, no matter had ever to human knowledge crossed this gulf of space, until early in the twentieth century this strange wanderer appeared. A vast mass of matter it was, bulky, heavy, rushing without warning out of the black mystery of the sky into the radiance of the sun. By the second day it was clearly visible to any decent instrument, as a speck with a barely sensible diameter, in the constellation Leo near Regulus. In a little while an opera glass could attain it.

On the third day of the new year the newspaper readers of two hemispheres were made aware for the first time of the real importance of this unusual apparition in the heavens. "A Planetary Collision," one London paper headed the news, and proclaimed Duchaine's opinion that this strange new planet would probably collide with Neptune. The leader writers enlarged upon the topic; so that in most of the capitals of the world, on January 3rd, there was an expectation, however vague of some imminent phenomenon in the sky; and as the night followed the sunset round the globe, thousands of men turned their eyes skyward to see--the old familiar stars just as they had always been.

Until it was dawn in London and Pollux setting and the stars overhead grown pale. The Winter's dawn it was, a sickly filtering accumulation of daylight, and the light of gas and candles shone yellow in the windows to show where people were astir. But the yawning policeman saw the thing, the busy crowds in the markets stopped agape, workmen going to their work betimes, milkmen, the drivers of news-carts, dissipation going home jaded and pale, homeless wanderers, sentinels on their beats, and in the country, labourers trudging afield, poachers slinking home, all over the dusky quickening country it could be seen--and out at sea by seamen watching for the day--a great white star, come suddenly into the westward sky!

Brighter it was than any star in our skies; brighter than the evening star at its brightest. It still glowed out white and large, no mere twinkling spot of light, but a small round clear shining disc, an hour after the day had come. And where science has not reached, men stared and feared, telling one another of the wars and pestilences that are foreshadowed by these fiery signs in the Heavens. Sturdy Boers, dusky Hottentots, Gold Coast Negroes, Frenchmen, Spaniards, Portuguese, stood in the warmth of the sunrise watching the setting of this strange new star.

And in a hundred observatories there had been suppressed excitement, rising almost to shouting pitch, as the two remote bodies had rushed together; and a hurrying to and fro, to gather photographic apparatus and spectroscope, and this appliance and that, to record this novel astonishing sight, the destruction of a world. For it was a world, a sister planet of our earth, far greater than our earth indeed, that had so suddenly flashed into flaming death. Neptune it was, had been struck, fairly and squarely, by the strange planet from outer space and the heat of the concussion had incontinently turned two solid globes into one vast mass of incandescence. Round the world that day, two hours before the dawn, went the pallid great white star, fading only as it sank westward and the sun mounted above it. Everywhere men marvelled at it, but of all those who saw it none could have marvelled more than those sailors, habitual watchers of the stars, who far away at sea had heard nothing of its advent and saw it now rise like a pigmy moon and climb zenithward and hang overhead and sink westward with the passing of the night.

And when next it rose over Europe everywhere were crowds of watchers on hilly slopes, on house-roofs, in open spaces, staring eastward for the rising of the great new star. It rose with a white glow in front of it, like the glare of a white fire, and those who had seen it come into existence the night before cried out at the sight of it. "It is larger," they cried. "It is brighter!" And, indeed the moon a quarter full and sinking in the west was in its apparent size beyond comparison, but scarcely in all its breadth had it as much brightness now as the little circle of the strange new star.

"It is brighter!" cried the people clustering in the streets. But in the dim observatories the watchers held their breath and peered at one another IT IS NEARER," they said. "NEARER!"

And voice after voice repeated, "It is nearer," and the clicking telegraph took that up, and it trembled along telephone wires, and in a thousand cities grimy compositors fingered the type. "It is nearer." Men writing in offices, struck with a strange realisation, flung down their pens, men talking in a thousand places suddenly came upon a grotesque possibility in those words, "It is nearer." It hurried along wakening streets, it was shouted down the frost-stilled ways of quiet villages; men who had read these things from the throbbing tape stood in yellow-lit doorways shouting the news to the passersby. "It is nearer." Pretty women, flushed and glittering, heard the news told jestingly between the dances, and feigned an intelligent interest they did not feel. "Nearer! Indeed. How curious! How very, very clever people must be to find out things like that!"

Lonely tramps faring through the wintry night murmured those words to comfort themselves--looking skyward. "It has need to be nearer, for the night's as cold as charity. Don't seem much warmth from it if it IS nearer, all the same."

"What is a new star to me?" cried the weeping woman kneeling beside her dead.

The schoolboy, rising early for his examination work, puzzled it out for himself--with the great white star shining broad and bright through the frost-flowers of his window. "Centrifugal, centripetal," he said, with his chin on his fist. "Stop a planet in its flight, rob it of its centrifugal force, what then? Centripetal has it, and down it falls into the sun! And this--!

"Do WE come in the way? I wonder--"

The light of that day went the way of its brethren, and with the later watches of the frosty darkness rose the strange star again. And it was now so bright that the waxing moon seemed but a pale yellow ghost of itself, hanging huge in the sunset. In a South African City a great man had married, and the streets were alight to welcome his return with his bride. "Even the skies have illuminated," said the flatterer. Under Capricorn, two negro lovers, daring the wild beasts and evil spirits, for love of one another, crouched together in a cane brake where the fire-flies hovered. "That is our star," they whispered, and felt strangely comforted by the sweet brilliance of its light.

The master mathematician sat in his private room and pushed the papers from him. His calculations were already finished. In a small white phial there still remained a little of the drug that had kept him awake and active for four long nights. Each day, serene, explicit, patient as ever, he had given his lecture to his students, and then had come back at once to this momentous calculation. His face was grave, a little drawn and hectic from his drugged activity. For some time he seemed lost in thought. Then he went to the window, and the blind went up with a click. Half way up the sky, over the clustering roofs, chimneys and steeples of the city, hung the star.

He looked at it as one might look into the eyes of a brave enemy. "You may kill me," he said after a silence. "But I can hold you--and all the universe for that matter--in the grip of this little brain. I would not change. Even now."

He looked at the little phial. "There will be no need of sleep again," he said. The next day at noon--punctual to the minute, he entered his lecture theatre, put his hat on the end of the table as his habit was, and carefully selected a large piece of chalk. It was a joke among his students that he could not lecture without that piece of chalk to fumble in his fingers, and once he had been stricken to impotence by their hiding his supply. He came and looked under his grey eyebrows at the rising tiers of young fresh faces, and spoke with his accustomed studied commonness of phrasing. "Circumstances have arisen--circumstances beyond my control," he said and paused, "which will debar me from completing the course I had designed. It would seem, gentlemen, if I may put the thing clearly and briefly, that--Man has lived in vain."

The students glanced at one another. Had they heard aright? Mad? Raised eyebrows and grinning lips there were, but one or two faces remained intent upon his calm grey-fringed face. "It will be interesting," he was saying, "to devote this morning to an exposition, so far as I can make it clear to you, of the calculations that have led me to this conclusion. Let us assume--"

He turned towards the blackboard, meditating a diagram in the way that was usual to him. "What was that about 'lived in vain?'" whispered one student to another. "Listen," said the other, nodding towards the lecturer.

And presently they began to understand.

That night the star rose later, for its proper eastward motion had carried it some way across Leo towards Virgo, and its brightness was so great that the sky became a luminous blue as it rose, and every star was hidden in its turn, save only Jupiter near the zenith, Capella, Aldebaran, Sirius and the pointers of the Bear. It was very white and beautiful. In many parts of the world that night a pallid halo encircled it about. It was perceptibly larger; in the clear refractive sky of the tropics it seemed as if it were nearly a quarter the size of the moon. The frost was still on the ground in England, but the world was as brightly lit as if it were midsummer moonlight. One could see to read quite ordinary print by that cold clear light, and in the cities the lamps burnt yellow and wan.

And everywhere the world was awake that night, and throughout Christendom a sombre murmur hung in the keen air over the country side like the belling of bees in the heather, and this murmurous tumult grew to a clangour in the cities. It was the tolling of the bells in a million belfry towers and steeples, summoning the people to sleep no more, to sin no more, but to gather in their churches and pray. And overhead, growing larger and brighter as the earth rolled on its way and the night passed, rose the dazzling star.

And the streets and houses were alight in all the cities, the shipyards glared, and whatever roads led to high country were lit and crowded all night long. And in all the seas about the civilised lands, ships with throbbing engines, and ships with bellying sails, crowded with men and living creatures, were standing out to ocean and the north. For already the warning of the master mathematician had been telegraphed all over the world, and translated into a hundred tongues. The new planet and Neptune, locked in a fiery embrace, were whirling headlong, ever faster and faster towards the sun. Already every second this blazing mass flew a hundred miles, and every second its terrific velocity increased. As it flew now, indeed, it must pass a hundred million of miles wide of the earth and scarcely affect it. But near its destined path, as yet only slightly perturbed, spun the mighty planet Jupiter and his moons sweeping splendid round the sun. Every moment now the attraction between the fiery star and the greatest of the planets grew stronger. And the result of that attraction? Inevitably Jupiter would be deflected from its orbit into an elliptical path, and the burning star, swung by his attraction wide of its sunward rush, would "describe a curved path" and perhaps collide with, and certainly pass very close to, our earth. "Earthquakes, volcanic outbreaks, cyclones, sea waves, floods, and a steady rise in temperature to I know not what limit"--so prophesied the master mathematician.

And overhead, to carry out his words, lonely and cold and livid, blazed the star of the coming doom.

To many who stared at it that night until their eyes ached, it seemed that it was visibly approaching. And that night, too, the weather changed, and the frost that had gripped all Central Europe and France and England softened towards a thaw.

But you must not imagine because I have spoken of people praying through the night and people going aboard ships and people fleeing toward mountainous country that the whole world was already in a terror because of the star. As a matter of fact, use and wont still ruled the world, and save for the talk of idle moments and the splendour of the night, nine human beings out of ten were still busy at their common occupations. In all the cities the shops, save one here and there, opened and closed at their proper hours, the doctor and the undertaker plied their trades, the workers gathered in the factories, soldiers drilled, scholars studied, lovers sought one another, thieves lurked and fled, politicians planned their schemes. The presses of the newspapers roared through the night, and many a priest of this church and that would not open his holy building to further what he considered a foolish panic. The newspapers insisted on the lesson of the year 1000--for then, too, people had anticipated the end. The star was no star--mere gas--a comet; and were it a star it could not possibly strike the earth. There was no precedent for such a thing. Common sense was sturdy everywhere, scornful, jesting, a little inclined to persecute the obdurate fearful. That night, at seven-fifteen by Greenwich time, the star would be at its nearest to Jupiter. Then the world would see the turn things would take. The master mathematician's grim warnings were treated by many as so much mere elaborate self-advertisement. Common sense at last, a little heated by argument, signified its unalterable convictions by going to bed. So, too, barbarism and savagery, already tired of the novelty, went about their nightly business, and save for a howling dog here and there, the beast world left the star unheeded.

And yet, when at last the watchers in the European States saw the star rise, an hour later it is true, but no larger than it had been the night before, there were still plenty awake to laugh at the master mathematician--to take the danger as if it had passed.

But hereafter the laughter ceased. The star grew--it grew with a terrible steadiness hour after hour, a little larger each hour, a little nearer the midnight zenith, and brighter and brighter, until it had turned night into a second day. Had it come straight to the earth instead of in a curved path, had it lost no velocity to Jupiter, it must have leapt the intervening gulf in a day, but as it was it took five days altogether to come by our planet. The next night it had become a third the size of the moon before it set to English eyes, and the thaw was assured. It rose over America near the size of the moon, but blinding white to look at, and HOT; and a breath of hot wind blew now with its rising and gathering strength, and in Virginia, and Brazil, and down the St. Lawrence valley, it shone intermittently through a driving reek of thunder-clouds, flickering violet lightning, and hail unprecedented. In Manitoba was a thaw and devastating floods. And upon all the mountains of the earth the snow and ice began to melt that night, and all the rivers coming out of high country flowed thick and turbid, and soon--in their upper reaches --with swirling trees and the bodies of beasts and men. They rose steadily, steadily in the ghostly brilliance, and came trickling over their banks at last, behind the flying population of their valleys.

And along the coast of Argentina and up the South Atlantic the tides were higher than had ever been in the memory of man, and the storms drove the waters in many cases scores of miles inland, drowning whole cities. And so great grew the heat during the night that the rising of the sun was like the coming of a shadow. The earthquakes began and grew until all down America from the Arctic Circle to Cape Horn, hillsides were sliding, fissures were opening, and houses and walls crumbling to destruction. The whole side of Cotopaxi slipped out in one vast convulsion, and a tumult of lava poured out so high and broad and swift and liquid that in one day it reached the sea.

So the star, with the wan moon in its wake, marched across the Pacific, trailed the thunderstorms like the hem of a robe, and the growing tidal wave that toiled behind it, frothing and eager, poured over island and island and swept them clear of men. Until that wave came at last--in a blinding light and with the breath of a furnace, swift and terrible it came--a wall of water, fifty feet high, roaring hungrily, upon the long coasts of Asia, and swept inland across the plains of China. For a space the star, hotter now and larger and brighter than the sun in its strength, showed with pitiless brilliance the wide and populous country; towns and villages with their pagodas and trees, roads, wide cultivated fields, millions of sleepless people staring in helpless terror at the incandescent sky; and then, low and growing, came the murmur of the flood. And thus it was with millions of men that night--a flight nowhither, with limbs heavy with heat and breath fierce and scant, and the flood like a wall swift and white behind. And then death.

China was lit glowing white, but over Japan and Java and all the islands of Eastern Asia the great star was a ball of dull red fire because of the steam and smoke and ashes the volcanoes were spouting forth to salute its coming. Above was the lava, hot gases and ash, and below the seething floods, and the whole earth swayed and rumbled with the earthquake shocks. Soon the immemorial snows of Thibet and the Himalaya were melting and pouring down by ten million deepening converging channels upon the plains of Burmah and Hindostan. The tangled summits of the Indian jungles were aflame in a thousand places, and below the hurrying waters around the stems were dark objects that still struggled feebly and reflected the blood-red tongues of fire. And in a rudderless confusion a multitude of men and women fled down the broad river-ways to that one last hope of men--the open sea.

Larger grew the star, and larger, hotter, and brighter with a terrible swiftness now. The tropical ocean had lost its phosphorescence, and the whirling steam rose in ghostly wreaths from the black waves that plunged incessantly, speckled with storm-tossed ships.

And then came a wonder. It seemed to those who in Europe watched for the rising of the star that the world must have ceased its rotation. In a thousand open spaces of down and upland the people who had fled thither from the floods and the falling houses and sliding slopes of hill watched for that rising in vain. Hour followed hour through a terrible suspense, and the star rose not. Once again men set their eyes upon the old constellations they had counted lost to them forever. In England it was hot and clear overhead, though the ground quivered perpetually, but in the tropics, Sirius and Capella and Aldebaran showed through a veil of steam. And when at last the great star rose near ten hours late, the sun rose close upon it, and in the centre of its white heart was a disc of black.

Over Asia it was the star had begun to fall behind the movement of the sky, and then suddenly, as it hung over India, its light had been veiled. All the plain of India from the mouth of the Indus to the mouths of the Ganges was a shallow waste of shining water that night, out of which rose temples and palaces, mounds and hills, black with people. Every minaret was a clustering mass of people, who fell one by one into the turbid waters, as heat and terror overcame them. The whole land seemed a-wailing and suddenly there swept a shadow across that furnace of despair, and a breath of cold wind, and a gathering of clouds, out of the cooling air. Men looking up, near blinded, at the star, saw that a black disc was creeping across the light. It was the moon, coming between the star and the earth. And even as men cried to God at this respite, out of the East with a strange inexplicable swiftness sprang the sun. And then star, sun and moon rushed together across the heavens.

So it was that presently, to the European watchers, star and sun rose close upon each other, drove headlong for a space and then slower, and at last came to rest, star and sun merged into one glare of flame at the zenith of the sky. The moon no longer eclipsed the star but was lost to sight in the brilliance of the sky. And though those who were still alive regarded it for the most part with that dull stupidity that hunger, fatigue, heat and despair engender, there were still men who could perceive the meaning of these signs. Star and earth had been at their nearest, had swung about one another, and the star had passed. Already it was receding, swifter and swifter, in the last stage of its headlong journey downward into the sun.

And then the clouds gathered, blotting out the vision of the sky, the thunder and lightning wove a garment round the world; all over the earth was such a downpour of rain as men had never before seen, and where the volcanoes flared red against the cloud canopy there descended torrents of mud. Everywhere the waters were pouring off the land, leaving mud-silted ruins, and the earth littered like a storm-worn beach with all that had floated, and the dead bodies of the men and brutes, its children. For days the water streamed off the land, sweeping away soil and trees and houses in the way, and piling huge dykes and scooping out Titanic gullies over the country side. Those were the days of darkness that followed the star and the heat. All through them, and for many weeks and months, the earthquakes continued.

But the star had passed, and men, hunger-driven and gathering courage only slowly, might creep back to their ruined cities, buried granaries, and sodden fields. Such few ships as had escaped the storms of that time came stunned and shattered and sounding their way cautiously through the new marks and shoals of once familiar ports. And as the storms subsided men perceived that everywhere the days were hotter than of yore, and the sun larger, and the moon, shrunk to a third of its former size, took now fourscore days between its new and new.

But of the new brotherhood that grew presently among men, of the saving of laws and books and machines, of the strange change that had come over Iceland and Greenland and the shores of Baffin's Bay, so that the sailors coming there presently found them green and gracious, and could scarce believe their eyes, this story does not tell. Nor of the movement of mankind now that the earth was hotter, northward and southward towards the poles of the earth. It concerns itself only with the coming and the passing of the Star.

The Martian astronomers--for there are astronomers on Mars, although they are very different beings from men--were naturally profoundly interested by these things. They saw them from their own standpoint of course. "Considering the mass and temperature of the missile that was flung through our solar system into the sun," one wrote, "it is astonishing what a little damage the earth, which it missed so narrowly, has sustained. All the familiar continental markings and the masses of the seas remain intact, and indeed the only difference seems to be a shrinkage of the white discoloration (supposed to be frozen water) round either pole." Which only shows how small the vastest of human catastrophes may seem, at a distance of a few million miles.

A DREAM OF ARMAGEDDON.

The man with the white face entered the carriage at Rugby. He moved slowly in spite of the urgency of his porter, and even while he was still on the platform I noted how ill he seemed. He dropped into the corner over against me with a sigh, made an incomplete attempt to arrange his travelling shawl, and became motionless, with his eyes staring vacantly. Presently he was moved by a sense of my observation, looked up at me, and put out a spiritless hand for his newspaper. Then he glanced again in my direction.

I feigned to read. I feared I had unwittingly embarrassed him, and in a moment I was surprised to find him speaking.

"I beg your pardon?" said I.

"That book," he repeated, pointing a lean finger, "is about dreams."

"Obviously," I answered, for it was Fortnum Roscoe's Dream States, and the title was on the cover.

He hung silent for a space as if he sought words. "Yes," he said at last, "but they tell you nothing."

I did not catch his meaning for a second.

"They don't know," he added.

I looked a little more attentively at his face.

"There are dreams," he said, "and dreams."

That sort of proposition I never dispute.

"I suppose--" he hesitated. "Do you ever dream? I mean vividly."

"I dream very little," I answered. "I doubt if I have three vivid dreams in a year."

"Ah!" he said, and seemed for a moment to collect his thoughts.

"Your dreams don't mix with your memories?" he asked abruptly.

"You don't find yourself in doubt; did this happen or did it not?"

"Hardly ever. Except just for a momentary hesitation now and then. I suppose few people do."

"Does he say--?" He indicated the book.

"Says it happens at times and gives the usual explanation about intensity of impression and the like to account for its not happening as a rule. I suppose you know something of these theories--"

"Very little--except that they are wrong."

His emaciated hand played with the strap of the window for a time. I prepared to resume reading, and that seemed to precipitate his next remark. He leant forward almost as though he would touch me.

"Isn't there something called consecutive dreaming--that goes on night after night?"

"I believe there is. There are cases given in most books on mental trouble."

"Mental trouble! Yes. I daresay there are. It's the right place for them. But what I mean--" He looked at his bony knuckles. "Is that sort of thing always dreaming? Is it dreaming?

Or is it something else? Mightn't it be something else?"

I should have snubbed his persistent conversation but for the drawn anxiety of his face. I remember now the look of his faded eyes and the lids red stained--perhaps you know that look.

"I'm not just arguing about a matter of opinion," he said. "The thing's killing me."

"Dreams?"

"If you call them dreams. Night after night. Vivid!--so vivid . . . . this--" (he indicated the landscape that went streaming by the window) "seems unreal in comparison! I can scarcely remember who I am, what business I am on . . . ."

He paused. "Even now--"

"The dream is always the same--do you mean?" I asked.

"It's over."

"You mean?"

"I died."

"Died?"

"Smashed and killed, and now, so much of me as that dream was, is dead. Dead forever. I dreamt I was another man, you know, living in a different part of the world and in a different time. I dreamt that night after night. Night after night I woke into that other life. Fresh scenes and fresh happenings--until I came upon the last--"

"When you died?"

"When I died."

"And since then--"

"No," he said. "Thank God! That was the end of the dream . . . "

It was clear I was in for this dream. And after all, I had an hour before me, the light was fading fast, and Fortnum Roscoe has a dreary way with him. "Living in a different time," I said: "do you mean in some different age?"

"Yes."

"Past?"

"No, to come--to come."

"The year three thousand, for example?"

"I don't know what year it was. I did when I was asleep, when I was dreaming, that is, but not now--not now that I am awake. There's a lot of things I have forgotten since I woke out of these dreams, though I knew them at the time when I was--I suppose it was dreaming. They called the year differently from our way of calling the year . . . What did they call it?" He put his hand to his forehead. "No," said he, "I forget."

He sat smiling weakly. For a moment I feared he did not mean to tell me his dream. As a rule I hate people who tell their dreams, but this struck me differently. I proffered assistance even. "It began--" I suggested.

"It was vivid from the first. I seemed to wake up in it suddenly. And it's curious that in these dreams I am speaking of I never remembered this life I am living now. It seemed as if the dream life was enough while it lasted. Perhaps--But I will tell you how I find myself when I do my best to recall it all. I don't remember anything clearly until I found myself sitting in a sort of loggia looking out over the sea. I had been dozing, and suddenly I woke up--fresh and vivid--not a bit dreamlike--because the girl had stopped fanning me."

"The girl?"

"Yes, the girl. You must not interrupt or you will put me out."

He stopped abruptly. "You won't think I'm mad?" he said.

"No," I answered. "You've been dreaming. Tell me your dream."

"I woke up, I say, because the girl had stopped fanning me. I was not surprised to find myself there or anything of that sort, you understand. I did not feel I had fallen into it suddenly. I simply took it up at that point. Whatever memory I had of this life, this nineteenth-century life, faded as I woke, vanished like a dream. I knew all about myself, knew that my name was no longer Cooper but Hedon, and all about my position in the world. I've forgotten a lot since I woke--there's a want of connection--but it was all quite clear and matter of fact then."

He hesitated again, gripping the window strap, putting his face forward and looking up to me appealingly.

"This seems bosh to you?"

"No, no!" I cried. "Go on. Tell me what this loggia was like!"

"It was not really a loggia--I don't know what to call it. It faced south. It was small. It was all in shadow except the semicircle above the balcony that showed the sky and sea and the corner where the girl stood. I was on a couch--it was a metal couch with light striped cushions--and the girl was leaning over the balcony with her back to me. The light of the sunrise fell on her ear and cheek. Her pretty white neck and the little curls that nestled there, and her white shoulder were in the sun, and all the grace of her body was in the cool blue shadow. She was dressed --how can I describe it? It was easy and flowing. And altogether there she stood, so that it came to me how beautiful and desirable she was, as though I had never seen her before. And when at last I sighed and raised myself upon my arm she turned her face to me--"

He stopped.

"I have lived three-and-fifty years in this world. I have had mother, sisters, friends, wife and daughters--all their faces, the play of their faces, I know. But the face of this girl--it is much more real to me. I can bring it back into memory so that I see it again--I could draw it or paint it. And after all--"

He stopped--but I said nothing.

"The face of a dream--the face of a dream. She was beautiful.

Not that beauty which is terrible, cold, and worshipful, like the beauty of a saint; nor that beauty that stirs fierce passions; but a sort of radiation, sweet lips that softened into smiles, and grave gray eyes. And she moved gracefully, she seemed to have part with all pleasant and gracious things--"

He stopped, and his face was downcast and hidden. Then he looked up at me and went on, making no further attempt to disguise his absolute belief in the reality of his story.

"You see, I had thrown up my plans and ambitions, thrown up all I had ever worked for or desired for her sake. I had been a master man away there in the north, with influence and property and a great reputation, but none of it had seemed worth having beside her. I had come to the place, this city of sunny pleasures with her, and left all those things to wreck and ruin just to save a remnant at least of my life. While I had been in love with her before I knew that she had any care for me, before I had imagined that she would dare--that we should dare, all my life had seemed vain and hollow, dust and ashes. It was dust and ashes. Night after night and through the long days I had longed and desired--my soul had beaten against the thing forbidden!

"But it is impossible for one man to tell another just these things. It's emotion, it's a tint, a light that comes and goes. Only while it's there, everything changes, everything. The thing is I came away and left them in their Crisis to do what they could."

"Left whom?" I asked, puzzled.

"The people up in the north there. You see--in this dream, anyhow--I had been a big man, the sort of man men come to trust in, to group themselves about. Millions of men who had never seen me were ready to do things and risk things because of their confidence in me. I had been playing that game for years, that big laborious game, that vague, monstrous political game amidst intrigues and betrayals, speech and agitation. It was a vast weltering world, and at last I had a sort of leadership against the Gang--you know it was called the Gang--a sort of compromise of scoundrelly projects and base ambitions and vast public emotional stupidities and catch-words--the Gang that kept the world noisy and blind year by year, and all the while that it was drifting, drifting towards infinite disaster. But I can't expect you to understand the shades and complications of the year--the year something or other ahead. I had it all--down to the smallest details--in my dream. I suppose I had been dreaming of it before I awoke, and the fading outline of some queer new development I had imagined still hung about me as I rubbed my eyes. It was some grubby affair that made me thank God for the sunlight. I sat up on the couch and remained looking at the woman and rejoicing--rejoicing that I had come away out of all that tumult and folly and violence before it was too late. After all, I thought, this is life--love and beauty, desire and delight, are they not worth all those dismal struggles for vague, gigantic ends? And I blamed myself for having ever sought to be a leader when I might have given my days to love. But then, thought I, if I had not spent my early days sternly and austerely, I might have wasted myself upon vain and worthless women, and at the thought all my being went out in love and tenderness to my dear mistress, my dear lady, who had come at last and compelled me--compelled me by her invincible charm for me--to lay that life aside.

"'You are worth it,' I said, speaking without intending her to hear; 'you are worth it, my dearest one; worth pride and praise and all things. Love! to have you is worth them all together." And at the murmur of my voice she turned about.

"'Come and see,' she cried--I can hear her now--'come and see the sunrise upon Monte Solaro.'

"I remember how I sprang to my feet and joined her at the balcony. She put a white hand upon my shoulder and pointed towards great masses of limestone, flushing, as it were, into life. I looked. But first I noted the sunlight on her face caressing the lines of her cheeks and neck. How can I describe to you the scene we had before us? We were at Capri--"

"I have been there," I said. "I have clambered up Monte Solaro and drunk vero Capri--muddy stuff like cider--at the summit."

"Ah!" said the man with the white face; "then perhaps you can tell me--you will know if this is indeed Capri. For in this life I have never been there. Let me describe it. We were in a little room, one of a vast multitude of little rooms, very cool and sunny, hollowed out of the limestone of a sort of cape, very high above the sea. The whole island, you know, was one enormous hotel, complex beyond explaining, and on the other side there were miles of floating hotels, and huge floating stages to which the flying machines came. They called it a pleasure city. Of course, there was none of that in your time--rather, I should say, is none of that now. Of course. Now!--yes.

"Well, this room of ours was at the extremity of the cape, so that one could see east and west. Eastward was a great cliff--a thousand feet high perhaps--coldly gray except for one bright edge of gold, and beyond it the Isle of the Sirens, and a falling coast that faded and passed into the hot sunrise. And when one turned to the west, distinct and near was a little bay, a little beach still in shadow. And out of that shadow rose Solaro straight and tall, flushed and golden crested, like a beauty throned, and the white moon was floating behind her in the sky. And before us from east to west stretched the many-tinted sea all dotted with little sailing boats.

"To the eastward, of course, these little boats were gray and very minute and clear, but to the westward they were little boats of gold--shining gold--almost like little flames. And just below us was a rock with an arch worn through it. The blue sea-water broke to green and foam all round the rock, and a galley came gliding out of the arch."

"I know that rock." I said. "I was nearly drowned there. It is called the Faraglioni."

"I Faraglioni? Yes, she called it that," answered the man with the white face. "There was some story--but that--"

He put his hand to his forehead again. " No," he said, "I forget that story."

"Well, that is the first thing I remember, the first dream I had, that little shaded room and the beautiful air and sky and that dear lady of mine, with her shining arms and her graceful robe, and how we sat and talked in half whispers to one another. We talked in whispers not because there was any one to hear, but because there was still such a freshness of mind between us that our thoughts were a little frightened, I think, to find themselves at last in words. And so they went softly.

"Presently we were hungry and we went from our apartment, going by a strange passage with a moving floor, until we came to the great breakfast room--there was a fountain and music. A pleasant and joyful place it was, with its sunlight and splashing, and the murmur of plucked strings. And we sat and ate and smiled at one another, and I would not heed a man who was watching me from a table near by.

"And afterwards we went on to the dancing-hall. But I cannot describe that hall. The place was enormous--larger than any building you have ever seen--and in one place there was the old gate of Capri, caught into the wall of a gallery high overhead. Light girders, stems and threads of gold, burst from the pillars like fountains, streamed like an Aurora across the roof and interlaced, like--like conjuring tricks. All about the great circle for the dancers there were beautiful figures, strange dragons, and intricate and wonderful grotesques bearing lights. The place was inundated with artificial light that shamed the newborn day. And as we went through the throng the people turned about and looked at us, for all through the world my name and face were known, and how I had suddenly thrown up pride and struggle to come to this place. And they looked also at the lady beside me, though half the story of how at last she had come to me was unknown or mistold. And few of the men who were there, I know, but judged me a happy man, in spite of all the shame and dishonour that had come upon my name.

"The air was full of music, full of harmonious scents, full of the rhythm of beautiful motions. Thousands of beautiful people swarmed about the hall, crowded the galleries, sat in a myriad recesses; they were dressed in splendid colours and crowned with flowers; thousands danced about the great circle beneath the white images of the ancient gods, and glorious processions of youths and maidens came and went. We two danced, not the dreary monotonies of your days--of this time, I mean--but dances that were beautiful, intoxicating. And even now I can see my lady dancing--dancing joyously. She danced, you know, with a serious face; she danced with a serious dignity, and yet she was smiling at me and caressing me--smiling and caressing with her eyes.

"The music was different," he murmured. "It went--I cannot describe it; but it was infinitely richer and more varied than any music that has ever come to me awake.

"And then--it was when we had done dancing--a man came to speak to me. He was a lean, resolute man, very soberly clad for that place, and already I had marked his face watching me in the breakfasting hall, and afterwards as we went along the passage I had avoided his eye. But now, as we sat in a little alcove, smiling at the pleasure of all the people who went to and fro across the shining floor, he came and touched me, and spoke to me so that I was forced to listen. And he asked that he might speak to me for a little time apart.

"'No,' I said. 'I have no secrets from this lady. What do you want to tell me?'

"He said it was a trivial matter, or at least a dry matter, for a lady to hear.

"'Perhaps for me to hear,' said I.

"He glanced at her, as though almost he would appeal to her. Then he asked me suddenly if I had heard of a great and avenging declaration that Evesham had made? Now, Evesham had always before been the man next to myself in the leadership of that great party in the north. He was a forcible, hard, and tactless man, and only I had been able to control and soften him. It was on his account even more than my own, I think, that the others had been so dismayed at my retreat. So this question about what he had done reawakened my old interest in the life I had put aside just for a moment.

"'I have taken no heed of any news for many days,' I said. 'What has Evesham been saying?'

"And with that the man began, nothing loth, and I must confess even I was struck by Evesham's reckless folly in the wild and threatening words he had used. And this messenger they had sent to me not only told me of Evesham's speech, but went on to ask counsel and to point out what need they had of me. While he talked, my lady sat a little forward and watched his face and mine.

"My old habits of scheming and organising reasserted themselves. I could even see myself suddenly returning to the north, and all the dramatic effect of it. All that this man said witnessed to the disorder of the party indeed, but not to its damage. I should go back stronger than I had come. And then I thought of my lady. You see--how can I tell you? There were certain peculiarities of our relationship--as things are I need not tell you about that--which would render her presence with me impossible. I should have had to leave her; indeed, I should have had to renounce her clearly and openly, if I was to do all that I could do in the north. And the man knew that, even as he talked to her and me, knew it as well as she did, that my steps to duty were--first, separation, then abandonment. At the touch of that thought my dream of a return was shattered. I turned on the man suddenly, as he was imagining his eloquence was gaining ground with me.

"'What have I to do with these things now?' I said. 'I have done with them. Do you think I am coquetting with your people in coming here?'

"'No,' he said. 'But--'

"'Why cannot you leave me alone. I have done with these things. I have ceased to be anything but a private man.'

"'Yes,' he answered. 'But have you thought?--this talk of war, these reckless challenges, these wild aggressions--'

"I stood up.

"'No,' I cried. 'I won't hear you. I took count of all those things, I weighed them--and I have come away.'

"He seemed to consider the possibility of persistence. He looked from me to where the lady sat regarding us.

"'War,' he said, as if he were speaking to himself, and then turned slowly from me and walked away.

"I stood, caught in the whirl of thoughts his appeal had set going.

"I heard my lady's voice.

"'Dear,' she said; 'but if they had need of you--'

"She did not finish her sentence, she let it rest there. I turned to her sweet face, and the balance of my mood swayed and reeled.

"'They want me only to do the thing they dare not do themselves,' I said. 'If they distrust Evesham they must settle with him themselves.'

"She looked at me doubtfully.

"'But war--' she said.

"I saw a doubt on her face that I had seen before, a doubt of herself and me, the first shadow of the discovery that, seen strongly and completely, must drive us apart for ever.

"Now, I was an older mind than hers, and I could sway her to this belief or that.

"'My dear one,' I said, 'you must not trouble over these things. There will be no war. Certainly there will be no war. The age of wars is past. Trust me to know the justice of this case. They have no right upon me, dearest, and no one has a right upon me. I have been free to choose my life, and I have chosen this.'

"'But war--,' she said.

"I sat down beside her. I put an arm behind her and took her hand in mine. I set myself to drive that doubt away--I set myself to fill her mind with pleasant things again. I lied to her, and in lying to her I lied also to myself. And she was only too ready to believe me, only too ready to forget.

"Very soon the shadow had gone again, and we were hastening to our bathing-place in the Grotta del Bovo Marino, where it was our custom to bathe every day. We swam and splashed one another, and in that buoyant water I seemed to become something lighter and stronger than a man. And at last we came out dripping and rejoicing and raced among the rocks. And then I put on a dry bathing-dress, and we sat to bask in the sun, and presently I nodded, resting my head against her knee, and she put her hand upon my hair and stroked it softly and I dozed. And behold! as it were with the snapping of the string of a violin, I was awakening, and I was in my own bed in Liverpool, in the life of to-day.

"Only for a time I could not believe that all these vivid moments had been no more than the substance of a dream.

"In truth, I could not believe it a dream for all the sobering reality of things about me. I bathed and dressed as it were by habit, and as I shaved I argued why I of all men should leave the woman I loved to go back to fantastic politics in the hard and strenuous north. Even if Evesham did force the world back to war, what was that to me? I was a man with the heart of a man, and why should I feel the responsibility of a deity for the way the world might go?

"You know that is not quite the way I think about affairs, about my real affairs. I am a solicitor, you know, with a point of view.

"The vision was so real, you must understand, so utterly unlike a dream that I kept perpetually recalling little irrelevant details; even the ornament of the book-cover that lay on my wife's sewing-machine in the breakfast-room recalled with the utmost vividness the gilt line that ran about the seat in the alcove where I had talked with the messenger from my deserted party. Have you ever heard of a dream that had a quality like that?"

"Like--?"

"So that afterwards you remembered little details you had forgotten."

I thought. I had never noticed the point before, but he was right.

"Never," I said. "That is what you never seem to do with dreams."

"No," he answered. "But that is just what I did. I am a solicitor, you must understand, in Liverpool, and I could not help wondering what the clients and business people I found myself talking to in my office would think if I told them suddenly I was in love with a girl who would be born a couple of hundred years or so hence, and worried about the politics of my great-great-great- grandchildren. I was chiefly busy that day negotiating a ninety-nine-year building lease. It was a private builder in a hurry, and we wanted to tie him in every possible way. I had an interview with him, and he showed a certain want of temper that sent me to bed still irritated. That night I had no dream. Nor did I dream the next night, at least, to remember.

"Something of that intense reality of conviction vanished. I began to feel sure it was a dream. And then it came again.

"When the dream came again, nearly four days later, it was very different. I think it certain that four days had also elapsed in the dream. Many things had happened in the north, and the shadow of them was back again between us, and this time it was not so easily dispelled. I began I know with moody musings. Why, in spite of all, should I go back, go back for all the rest of my days to toil and stress, insults and perpetual dissatisfaction, simply to save hundreds of millions of common people, whom I did not love, whom too often I could do no other than despise, from the stress and anguish of war and infinite misrule? And after all I might fail. They all sought their own narrow ends, and why should not I--why should not I also live as a man? And out of such thoughts her voice summoned me, and I lifted my eyes.

I found myself awake and walking. We had come out above the Pleasure City, we were near the summit of Monte Solaro and looking towards the bay. It was the late afternoon and very clear. Far away to the left Ischia hung in a golden haze between sea and sky, and Naples was coldly white against the hills, and before us was Vesuvius with a tall and slender streamer feathering at last towards the south, and the ruins of Torre dell' Annunziata and Castellammare glittering and near."

I interrupted suddenly: "You have been to Capri, of course?"

"Only in this dream," he said, "only in this dream. All across the bay beyond Sorrento were the floating palaces of the Pleasure City moored and chained. And northward were the broad floating stages that received the aeroplanes. Aeroplanes fell out of the sky every afternoon, each bringing its thousands of pleasure-seekers from the uttermost parts of the earth to Capri and its delights. All these things, I say, stretched below.

"But we noticed them only incidentally because of an unusual sight that evening had to show. Five war aeroplanes that had long slumbered useless in the distant arsenals of the Rhinemouth were manoeuvring now in the eastward sky. Evesham had astonished the world by producing them and others, and sending them to circle here and there. It was the threat material in the great game of bluff he was playing, and it had taken even me by surprise. He was one of those incredibly stupid energetic people who seem sent by heaven to create disasters. His energy to the first glance seemed so wonderfully like capacity! But he had no imagination, no invention, only a stupid, vast, driving force of will, and a mad faith in his stupid idiot 'luck' to pull him through. I remember how we stood upon the headland watching the squadron circling far away, and how I weighed the full meaning of the sight, seeing clearly the way things must go. And then even it was not too late.

I might have gone back, I think, and saved the world. The people of the north would follow me, I knew, granted only that in one thing I respected their moral standards. The east and south would trust me as they would trust no other northern man. And I knew I had only to put it to her and she would have let me go . . . . Not because she did not love me!

"Only I did not want to go; my will was all the other way about. I had so newly thrown off the incubus of responsibility: I was still so fresh a renegade from duty that the daylight clearness of what I ought to do had no power at all to touch my will. My will was to live, to gather pleasures and make my dear lady happy. But though this sense of vast neglected duties had no power to draw me, it could make me silent and preoccupied, it robbed the days I had spent of half their brightness and roused me into dark meditations in the silence of the night. And as I stood and watched Evesham's aeroplanes sweep to and fro--those birds of infinite ill omen--she stood beside me watching me, perceiving the trouble indeed, but not perceiving it clearly--her eyes questioning my face, her expression shaded with perplexity. Her face was gray because the sunset was fading out of the sky. It was no fault of hers that she held me. She had asked me to go from her, and again in the night time and with tears she had asked me to go.

"At last it was the sense of her that roused me from my mood. I turned upon her suddenly and challenged her to race down the mountain slopes. 'No,' she said, as if I had jarred with her gravity, but I was resolved to end that gravity, and make her run--no one can be very gray and sad who is out of breath--and when she stumbled I ran with my hand beneath her arm. We ran down past a couple of men, who turned back staring in astonishment at my behaviour--they must have recognised my face. And half way down the slope came a tumult in the air, clang-clank, clang-clank, and we stopped, and presently over the hill-crest those war things came flying one behind the other."

The man seemed hesitating on the verge of a description.

"What were they like?" I asked.

"They had never fought," he said. "They were just like our ironclads are nowadays; they had never fought. No one knew what they might do, with excited men inside them; few even cared to speculate. They were great driving things shaped like spear-heads without a shaft, with a propeller in the place of the shaft."

"Steel?"

"Not steel."

"Aluminum?"

"No, no, nothing of that sort. An alloy that was very common--as common as brass, for example. It was called--let me see--" He squeezed his forehead with the fingers of one hand. "I am forgetting everything," he said.

"And they carried guns?"

"Little guns, firing high explosive shells. They fired the guns backwards, out of the base of the leaf, so to speak, and rammed with the beak. That was the theory, you know, but they had never been fought. No one could tell exactly what was going to happen. And meanwhile I suppose it was very fine to go whirling through the air like a flight of young swallows, swift and easy. I guess the captains tried not to think too clearly what the real thing would be like. And these flying war machines, you know, were only one sort of the endless war contrivances that had been invented and had fallen into abeyance during the long peace. There were all sorts of these things that people were routing out and furbishing up; infernal things, silly things; things that had never been tried; big engines, terrible explosives, great guns. You know the silly way of these ingenious sort of men who make these things; they turn 'em out as beavers build dams, and with no more sense of the rivers they're going to divert and the lands they're going to flood!

"As we went down the winding stepway to our hotel again, in the twilight, I foresaw it all: I saw how clearly and inevitably things were driving for war in Evesham's silly, violent hands, and I had some inkling of what war was bound to be under these new conditions. And even then, though I knew it was drawing near the limit of my opportunity, I could find no will to go back."

He sighed.

"That was my last chance.

"We didn't go into the city until the sky was full of stars, so we walked out upon the high terrace, to and fro, and--she counselled me to go back.

"'My dearest,' she said, and her sweet face looked up to me, 'this is Death. This life you lead is Death. Go back to them, go back to your duty--'

"She began to weep, saying, between her sobs, and clinging to my arm as she said it, 'Go back--Go back.'

"Then suddenly she fell mute, and, glancing down at her face, I read in an instant the thing she had thought to do. It was one of those moments when one sees.

"'No!' I said.

"'No?' she asked, in surprise and I think a little fearful at the answer to her thought.

"'Nothing,' I said, 'shall send me back. Nothing! I have chosen. Love, I have chosen, and the world must go. Whatever happens I will live this life--I will live for you! It--nothing shall turn me aside; nothing, my dear one. Even if you died--even if you died--'

"'Yes?' she murmured, softly.

"'Then--I also would die.'

"And before she could speak again I began to talk, talking eloquently--as I could do in that life--talking to exalt love, to make the life we were living seem heroic and glorious; and the thing I was deserting something hard and enormously ignoble that it was a fine thing to set aside. I bent all my mind to throw that glamour upon it, seeking not only to convert her but myself to that. We talked, and she clung to me, torn too between all that she deemed noble and all that she knew was sweet. And at last I did make it heroic, made all the thickening disaster of the world only a sort of glorious setting to our unparalleled love, and we two poor foolish souls strutted there at last, clad in that splendid delusion, drunken rather with that glorious delusion, under the still stars.

"And so my moment passed.

"It was my last chance. Even as we went to and fro there, the leaders of the south and east were gathering their resolve, and the hot answer that shattered Evesham's bluffing for ever, took shape and waited. And, all over Asia, and the ocean, and the South, the air and the wires were throbbing with their warnings to prepare --prepare.

"No one living, you know, knew what war was; no one could imagine, with all these new inventions, what horror war might bring. I believe most people still believed it would be a matter of bright uniforms and shouting charges and triumphs and flags and bands--in a time when half the world drew its food supply from regions ten thousand miles away--"

The man with the white face paused. I glanced at him, and his face was intent on the floor of the carriage. A little railway station, a string of loaded trucks, a signal-box, and the back of a cottage, shot by the carriage window, and a bridge passed with a clap of noise, echoing the tumult of the train.

"After that," he said, "I dreamt often. For three weeks of nights that dream was my life. And the worst of it was there were nights when I could not dream, when I lay tossing on a bed in this accursed life; and there--somewhere lost to me--things were happening--momentous, terrible things . . . I lived at nights--my days, my waking days, this life I am living now, became a faded, far-away dream, a drab setting, the cover of the book."

He thought.

"I could tell you all, tell you every little thing in the dream, but as to what I did in the daytime--no. I could not tell--I do not remember. My memory--my memory has gone. The business of life slips from me--"

He leant forward, and pressed his hands upon his eyes. For a long time he said nothing.

"And then?" said I.

"The war burst like a hurricane."

He stared before him at unspeakable things.

"And then?" I urged again.

"One touch of unreality," he said, in the low tone of a man who speaks to himself," and they would have been nightmares. But they were not nightmares--they were not nightmares. No!"

He was silent for so long that it dawned upon me that there was a danger of losing the rest of the story. But he went on talking again in the same tone of questioning self-communion.

"What was there to do but flight? I had not thought the war would touch Capri--I had seemed to see Capri as being out of it all, as the contrast to it all; but two nights after the whole place was shouting and bawling, every woman almost and every other man wore a badge--Evesham's badge--and there was no music but a jangling war-song over and over again, and everywhere men enlisting, and in the dancing halls they were drilling. The whole island was awhirl with rumours; it was said, again and again, that fighting had begun. I had not expected this. I had seen so little of the life of pleasure that I had failed to reckon with this violence of the amateurs. And as for me, I was out of it. I was like the man who might have prevented the firing of a magazine. The time had gone. I was no one; the vainest stripling with a badge counted for more than I. The crowd jostled us and bawled in our ears; that accursed song deafened us; a woman shrieked at my lady because no badge was on her, and we two went back to our own place again, ruffled and insulted--my lady white and silent, and I aquiver with rage. So furious was I, I could have quarrelled with her if I could have found one shade of accusation in her eyes.

"All my magnificence had gone from me. I walked up and down our rock cell, and outside was the darkling sea and a light to the southward that flared and passed and came again.

"'We must get out of this place,' I said over and over. 'I have made my choice, and I will have no hand in these troubles. I will have nothing of this war. We have taken our lives out of all these things. This is no refuge for us. Let us go.'

"And the next day we were already in flight from the war that covered the world.

"And all the rest was Flight--all the rest was Flight."

He mused darkly.

"How much was there of it?"

He made no answer.

"How many days?"

His face was white and drawn and his hands were clenched. He took no heed of my curiosity.

I tried to draw him back to his story with questions.

"Where did you go?" I said.

"When?"

"When you left Capri."

"South-west," he said, and glanced at me for a second. "We went in a boat."

"But I should have thought an aeroplane?"

"They had been seized."

I questioned him no more. Presently I thought he was beginning again. He broke out in an argumentative monotone:

"But why should it be? If, indeed, this battle, this slaughter and stress is life, why have we this craving for pleasure and beauty? If there is no refuge, if there is no place of peace, and if all our dreams of quiet places are a folly and a snare, why have we such dreams? Surely it was no ignoble cravings, no base intentions, had brought us to this; it was Love had isolated us. Love had come to me with her eyes and robed in her beauty, more glorious than all else in life, in the very shape and colour of life, and summoned me away. I had silenced all the voices, I had answered all the questions--I had come to her. And suddenly there was nothing but War and Death!"

I had an inspiration. " After all," I said, "it could have been only a dream."

"A dream!" he cried, flaming upon me, "a dream--when, even now--"

For the first time he became animated. A faint flush crept into his cheek. He raised his open hand and clenched it, and dropped it to his knee. He spoke, looking away from me, and for all the rest of the time he looked away. "We are but phantoms!" he said, "and the phantoms of phantoms, desires like cloud-shadows and wills of straw that eddy in the wind; the days pass, use and wont carry us through as a train carries the shadow of its lights--so be it! But one thing is real and certain, one thing is no dream- stuff, but eternal and enduring. It is the centre of my life, and all other things about it are subordinate or altogether vain. I loved her, that woman of a dream. And she and I are dead together!

"A dream! How can it be a dream, when it drenched a living life with unappeasable sorrow, when it makes all that I have lived for and cared for, worthless and unmeaning?

"Until that very moment when she was killed I believed we had still a chance of getting away," he said. "All through the night and morning that we sailed across the sea from Capri to Salerno, we talked of escape. We were full of hope, and it clung about us to the end, hope for the life together we should lead, out of it all, out of the battle and struggle, the wild and empty passions, the empty arbitrary 'thou shalt' and 'thou shalt not' of the world. We were uplifted, as though our quest was a holy thing, as though love for another was a mission . . . .

"Even when from our boat we saw the fair face of that great rock Capri--already scarred and gashed by the gun emplacements and hiding-places that were to make it a fastness--we reckoned nothing of the imminent slaughter, though the fury of preparation hung about in the puffs and clouds of dust at a hundred points amidst the gray; but, indeed, I made a text of that and talked. There, you know, was the rock, still beautiful for all its scars, with its countless windows and arches and ways, tier upon tier, for a thousand feet, a vast carving of gray, broken by vine-clad terraces, and lemon and orange groves, and masses of agave and prickly pear, and puffs of almond blossom. And out under the archway that is built over the Piccola Marina other boats were coming; and as we came round the cape and within sight of the mainland, another little string of boats came into view, driving before the wind towards the south-west. In a little while a multitude had come out, the remoter just little specks of ultramarine in the shadow of the eastward cliff.

"'It is love and reason,' I said, 'fleeing from all this madness of war.'

"And though we presently saw a squadron of aeroplanes flying across the southern sky we did not heed it. There it was--a line of little dots in the sky--and then more, dotting the south-eastern horizon, and then still more, until all that quarter of the sky was stippled with blue specks. Now they were all thin little strokes of blue, and now one and now a multitude would heel and catch the sun and become short flashes of light. They came, rising and falling and growing larger, like some huge flight of gulls or rooks or such-like birds, moving with a marvellous uniformity, and ever as they drew nearer they spread over a greater width of sky. The southward wind flung itself in an arrow-headed cloud athwart the sun. And then suddenly they swept round to the eastward and streamed eastward, growing smaller and smaller and clearer and clearer again until they vanished from the sky. And after that we noted to the northward and very high Evesham's fighting machines hanging high over Naples like an evening swarm of gnats.

"It seemed to have no more to do with us than a flight of birds.

"Even the mutter of guns far away in the south-east seemed to us to signify nothing . . .

"Each day, each dream after that, we were still exalted, still seeking that refuge where we might live and love. Fatigue had come upon us, pain and many distresses. For though we were dusty and stained by our toilsome tramping, and half starved and with the horror of the dead men we had seen and the flight of the peasants--for very soon a gust of fighting swept up the peninsula--with these things haunting our minds it still resulted only in a deepening resolution to escape. Oh, but she was brave and patient! She who had never faced hardship and exposure had courage for herself and me. We went to and fro seeking an outlet, over a country all commandeered and ransacked by the gathering hosts of war. Always we went on foot. At first there were other fugitives, but we did not mingle with them. Some escaped northward, some were caught in the torrent of peasantry that swept along the main roads; many gave themselves into the hands of the soldiery and were sent northward. Many of the men were impressed. But we kept away from these things; we had brought no money to bribe a passage north, and I feared for my lady at the hands of these conscript crowds. We had landed at Salerno, and we had been turned back from Cava, and we had tried to cross towards Taranto by a pass over Mount Alburno, but we had been driven back for want of food, and so we had come down among the marshes by Paestum, where those great temples stand alone. I had some vague idea that by

Paestum it might be possible to find a boat or something, and take once more to sea. And there it was the battle overtook us.

"A sort of soul-blindness had me. Plainly I could see that we were being hemmed in; that the great net of that giant Warfare had us in its toils. Many times we had seen the levies that had come down from the north going to and fro, and had come upon them in the distance amidst the mountains making ways for the ammunition and preparing the mounting of the guns. Once we fancied they had fired at us, taking us for spies--at any rate a shot had gone shuddering over us. Several times we had hidden in woods from hovering aeroplanes.

"But all these things do not matter now, these nights of flight and pain . . . We were in an open place near those great temples at Paestum, at last, on a blank stony place dotted with spiky bushes, empty and desolate and so flat that a grove of eucalyptus far away showed to the feet of its stems. How I can see it! My lady was sitting down under a bush resting a little, for she was very weak and weary, and I was standing up watching to see if I could tell the distance of the firing that came and went. They were still, you know, fighting far from each other, with those terrible new weapons that had never before been used: guns that would carry beyond sight, and aeroplanes that would do--What they would do no man could foretell.

"I knew that we were between the two armies, and that they drew together. I knew we were in danger, and that we could not stop there and rest!

"Though all these things were in my mind, they were in the background. They seemed to be affairs beyond our concern. Chiefly, I was thinking of my lady. An aching distress filled me. For the first time she had owned herself beaten and had fallen a-weeping. Behind me I could hear her sobbing, but I would not turn round to her because I knew she had need of weeping, and had held herself so far and so long for me. It was well, I thought, that she would weep and rest and then we would toil on again, for I had no inkling of the thing that hung so near. Even now I can see her as she sat there, her lovely hair upon her shoulder, can mark again the deepening hollow of her cheek.

"'If we had parted,' she said, 'if I had let you go.'

"'No,' said I.' Even now, I do not repent. I will not repent; I made my choice, and I will hold on to the end.'

"And then--

"Overhead in the sky flashed something and burst, and all about us I heard the bullets making a noise like a handful of peas suddenly thrown. They chipped the stones about us, and whirled fragments from the bricks and passed . . . ."

He put his hand to his mouth, and then moistened his lips.

"At the flash I had turned about . . .

"You know--she stood up--

"She stood up, you know, and moved a step towards me--as though she wanted to reach me--

"And she had been shot through the heart."

He stopped and stared at me. I felt all that foolish incapacity an Englishman feels on such occasions. I met his eyes for a moment, and then stared out of the window. For a long space we kept silence. When at last I looked at him he was sitting back in his corner, his arms folded, and his teeth gnawing at his knuckles.

He bit his nail suddenly, and stared at it.

"I carried her," he said, "towards the temples, in my arms--as though it mattered. I don't know why. They seemed a sort of sanctuary, you know, they had lasted so long, I suppose.

"She must have died almost instantly. Only--I talked to her all the way."

Silence again.

"I have seen those temples," I said abruptly, and indeed he had brought those still, sunlit arcades of worn sandstone very vividly before me.

"It was the brown one, the big brown one. I sat down on a fallen pillar and held her in my arms . . . Silent after the first babble was over. And after a little while the lizards came out and ran about again, as though nothing unusual was going on, as though nothing had changed . . . It was tremendously still there, the sun high and the shadows still; even the shadows of the weeds upon the entablature were still--in spite of the thudding and banging that went all about the sky.

"I seem to remember that the aeroplanes came up out of the south, and that the battle went away to the west. One aeroplane was struck, and overset and fell. I remember that--though it didn't interest me in the least. It didn't seem to signify. It was like a wounded gull, you know--flapping for a time in the water. I could see it down the aisle of the temple--a black thing in the bright blue water.

"Three or four times shells burst about the beach, and then that ceased. Each time that happened all the lizards scuttled in and hid for a space. That was all the mischief done, except that once a stray bullet gashed the stone hard by--made just a fresh bright surface.

"As the shadows grew longer, the stillness seemed greater.

"The curious thing," he remarked, with the manner of a man who makes a trivial conversation, "is that I didn't THINK--at all. I sat with her in my arms amidst the stones--in a sort of lethargy--stagnant.

"And I don't remember waking up. I don't remember dressing that day. I know I found myself in my office, with my letters all slit open in front of me, and how I was struck by the absurdity of being there, seeing that in reality I was sitting, stunned, in that Paestum Temple with a dead woman in my arms. I read my letters like a machine. I have forgotten what they were about."

He stopped, and there was a long silence.

Suddenly I perceived that we were running down the incline from Chalk Farm to Euston. I started at this passing of time. I turned on him with a brutal question, with the tone of "Now or never."

"And did you dream again?"

"Yes."

He seemed to force himself to finish. His voice was very low.

"Once more, and as it were only for a few instants. I seemed to have suddenly awakened out of a great apathy, to have risen into a sitting position, and the body lay there on the stones beside me.

A gaunt body. Not her, you know. So soon--it was not her . . . .

"I may have heard voices. I do not know. Only I knew clearly that men were coming into the solitude and that that was a last outrage.

"I stood up and walked through the temple, and then there came into sight--first one man with a yellow face, dressed in a uniform of dirty white, trimmed with blue, and then several, climbing to the crest of the old wall of the vanished city, and crouching there. They were little bright figures in the sunlight, and there they hung, weapon in hand, peering cautiously before them.

"And further away I saw others and then more at another point in the wall. It was a long lax line of men in open order.

"Presently the man I had first seen stood up and shouted a command, and his men came tumbling down the wall and into the high weeds towards the temple. He scrambled down with them and led them. He came facing towards me, and when he saw me he stopped.

"At first I had watched these men with a mere curiosity, but when I had seen they meant to come to the temple I was moved to forbid them. I shouted to the officer.

"'You must not come here,' I cried, '*I* am here. I am here with my dead.'

"He stared, and then shouted a question back to me in some unknown tongue.

"I repeated what I had said.

"He shouted again, and I folded my arms and stood still. Presently he spoke to his men and came forward. He carried a drawn sword.

"I signed to him to keep away, but he continued to advance. I told him again very patiently and clearly: 'You must not come here. These are old temples and I am here with my dead.'

"Presently he was so close I could see his face clearly. It was a narrow face, with dull gray eyes, and a black moustache. He had a scar on his upper lip, and he was dirty and unshaven. He kept shouting unintelligible things, questions, perhaps, at me.

"I know now that he was afraid of me, but at the time that did not occur to me. As I tried to explain to him, he interrupted me in imperious tones, bidding me, I suppose, stand aside.

"He made to go past me, and I caught hold of him.

"I saw his face change at my grip.

"'You fool,' I cried. 'Don't you know? She is dead!'

"He started back. He looked at me with cruel eyes. I saw a sort of exultant resolve leap into them--delight. Then, suddenly, with a scowl, he swept his sword back--SO--and thrust."

He stopped abruptly.

I became aware of a change in the rhythm of the train. The brakes lifted their voices and the carriage jarred and jerked. This present world insisted upon itself, became clamourous. I saw through the steamy window huge electric fights glaring down from tall masts upon a fog, saw rows of stationary empty carriages passing by, and then a signal-box hoisting its constellation of green and red into the murky London twilight, marched after them. I looked again at his drawn features.

"He ran me through the heart. It was with a sort of astonishment--no fear, no pain--but just amazement, that I felt it pierce me, felt the sword drive home into my body. It didn't hurt, you know. It didn't hurt at all."

The yellow platform lights came into the field of view, passing first rapidly, then slowly, and at last stopping with a jerk. Dim shapes of men passed to and fro without.

"Euston!" cried a voice.

"Do you mean--?"

"There was no pain, no sting or smart. Amazement and then darkness sweeping over everything. The hot, brutal face before me, the face of the man who had killed me, seemed to recede. It swept out of existence--"

"Euston!" clamoured the voices outside; "Euston!"

The carriage door opened admitting a flood of sound, and a porter stood regarding us. The sounds of doors slamming, and the hoof-clatter of cab-horses, and behind these things the featureless remote roar of the London cobble-stones, came to my ears. A truckload of lighted lamps blazed along the platform.

"A darkness, a flood of darkness that opened and spread and blotted out all things."

"Any luggage, sir?" said the porter.

"And that was the end?" I asked.

He seemed to hesitate. Then, almost inaudibly, he answered, "NO."

"You mean?"

"I couldn't get to her. She was there on the other side of the temple-- And then--"

"Yes," I insisted. "Yes?"

"Nightmares," he cried; "nightmares indeed! My God! Great birds that fought and tore."

THE CONE.

The night was hot and overcast, the sky red, rimmed with the lingering sunset of mid-summer. They sat at the open window, trying to fancy the air was fresher there. The trees and shrubs of the garden stood stiff and dark; beyond in the roadway a gas-lamp burnt, bright orange against the hazy blue of the evening. Farther were the three lights of the railway signal against the lowering sky. The man and woman spoke to one another in low tones.

"He does not suspect?" said the man, a little nervously.

"Not he," she said peevishly, as though that too irritated her. "He thinks of nothing but the works and the prices of fuel. He has no imagination, no poetry."

"None of these men of iron have," he said sententiously. "They have no hearts."

"HE has not," she said. She turned her discontented face towards the window. The distant sound of a roaring and rushing drew nearer and grew in volume; the house quivered; one heard the metallic rattle of the tender. As the train passed, there was a glare of light above the cutting and a driving tumult of smoke; one, two, three, four, five, six, seven, eight black oblongs--eight trucks--passed across the dim grey of the embankment, and were suddenly extinguished one by one in the throat of the tunnel, which, with the last, seemed to swallow down train, smoke, and sound in one abrupt gulp.

"This country was all fresh and beautiful once," he said; "and now--it is Gehenna. Down that way--nothing but pot-banks and chimneys belching fire and dust into the face of heaven . . . . . But what does it matter? An end comes, an end to all this cruelty . . . . . TO-MORROW." He spoke the last word in a whisper.

"TO-MORROW," she said, speaking in a whisper too, and still staring out of the window.

"Dear!" he said, putting his hand on hers.

She turned with a start, and their eyes searched one another's. Hers softened to his gaze. "My dear one!" she said, and then: "It seems so strange --that you should have come into my life like this--to open--" She paused.

"To open?" he said.

"All this wonderful world--" she hesitated, and spoke still more softly--"this world of LOVE to me."

Then suddenly the door clicked and closed. They turned their heads, and he started violently back. In the shadow of the room stood a great shadowy figure--silent. They saw the face dimly in the half-light, with unexpressive dark patches under the penthouse brows. Every muscle in Raut's body suddenly became tense. When could the door have opened? What had he heard? Had he heard all? What had he seen? A tumult of questions.

The new-comer's voice came at last, after a pause that seemed interminable. "Well?" he said.

"I was afraid I had missed you, Horrocks," said the man at the window, gripping the window-ledge with his hand. His voice was unsteady.

The clumsy figure of Horrocks came forward out of the shadow. He made no answer to Raut's remark. For a moment he stood above them.

The woman's heart was cold within her. "I told Mr. Raut it was just possible you might come back," she said, in a voice that never quivered.

Horrocks, still silent, sat down abruptly in the chair by her little work-table. His big hands were clenched; one saw now the fire of his eyes under the shadow of his brows. He was trying to get his breath. His eyes went from the woman he had trusted to the friend he had trusted, and then back to the woman.

By this time and for the moment all three half understood one another. Yet none dared say a word to ease the pent-up things that choked them.

It was the husband's voice that broke the silence at last.

"You wanted to see me?" he said to Raut.

Raut started as he spoke. "I came to see you," he said, resolved to lie to the last.

"Yes," said Horrocks.

"You promised," said Raut, "to show me some fine effects of moonlight and smoke."

"I promised to show you some fine effects of moonlight and smoke," repeated Horrocks in a colourless voice.

"And I thought I might catch you to-night before you went down to the works," proceeded Raut, "and come with you."

There was another pause. Did the man mean to take the thing coolly? Did he after all know? How long had he been in the room? Yet even at the moment when they heard the door, their attitudes . . . . Horrocks glanced at the profile of the woman, shadowy pallid in the half-light. Then he glanced at Raut, and seemed to recover himself suddenly. "Of course," he said, "I promised to show you the works under their proper dramatic conditions. It's odd how I could have forgotten."

"If I am troubling you--" began Raut.

Horrocks started again. A new light had suddenly come into the sultry gloom of his eyes. "Not in the least," he said.

"Have you been telling Mr. Raut of all these contrasts of flame and shadow you think so splendid?" said the woman, turning now to her husband for the first time, her confidence creeping back again, her voice just one half-note too high. "That dreadful theory of yours that machinery is beautiful, and everything else in the world ugly. I thought he would not spare you, Mr. Raut. It's his great theory, his one discovery in art."

"I am slow to make discoveries," said Horrocks grimly, damping her suddenly. "But what I discover . . . . ." He stopped.

"Well?" she said.

"Nothing;" and suddenly he rose to his feet.

"I promised to show you the works," he said to Raut, and put his big, clumsy hand on his friend's shoulder. "And you are ready to go?"

"Quite," said Raut, and stood up also.

There was another pause. Each of them peered through the indistinctness of the dusk at the other two. Horrocks' hand still rested on Raut's shoulder. Raut half fancied still that the incident was trivial after all. But Mrs. Horrocks knew her husband better, knew that grim quiet in his voice, and the confusion in her mind took a vague shape of physical evil. "Very well", said Horrocks, and, dropping his hand, turned towards the door.

"My hat?" Raut looked round in the half-light.

"That's my work-basket," said Mrs. Horrocks, with a gust of hysterical laughter. Their hands came together on the back of the chair. "Here it is!" he said. She had an impulse to warn him in an undertone, but she could not frame a word. "Don't go!" and "Beware of him!" struggled in her mind, and the swift moment passed.

"Got it?" said Horrocks, standing with the door half open.

Raut stepped towards him. "Better say good-bye to Mrs. Horrocks," said the ironmaster, even more grimly quiet in his tone than before.

Raut started and turned. "Good-evening, Mrs. Horrocks," he said, and their hands touched.

Horrocks held the door open with a ceremonial politeness unusual in him towards men. Raut went out, and then, after a wordless look at her, her husband followed. She stood motionless while Raut's light footfall and her husband's heavy tread, like bass and treble, passed down the passage together. The front door slammed heavily. She went to the window, moving slowly, and stood watching--leaning forward. The two men appeared for a moment at the gateway in the road, passed under the street lamp, and were hidden by the black masses of the shrubbery. The lamp-light fell for a moment on their faces, showing only unmeaning pale patches, telling nothing of what she still feared, and doubted, and craved vainly to know. Then she sank down into a crouching attitude in the big arm-chair, her eyes wide open and staring out at the red lights from the furnaces that flickered in the sky. An hour after she was still there, her attitude scarcely changed.

The oppressive stillness of the evening weighed heavily upon Raut. They went side by side down the road in silence, and in silence turned into the cinder-made by-way that presently opened out the prospect of the valley.

A blue haze, half dust, half mist, touched the long valley with mystery. Beyond were Hanley and Etruria, grey and dark masses, outlined thinly by the rare golden dots of the street lamps, and here and there a gaslit window, or the yellow glare of some late-working factory or crowded public-house. Out of the masses, clear and slender against the evening sky, rose a multitude of tall chimneys, many of them reeking, a few smokeless during a season of "play." Here and there a pallid patch and ghostly stunted beehive shapes showed the position of a pot-bank, or a wheel, black and sharp against the hot lower sky, marked some colliery where they raise the iridescent coal of the place. Nearer at hand was the broad stretch of railway, and half invisible trains shunted--a steady puffing and rumbling, with every run a ringing concussion and a rhythmic series of impacts, and a passage of intermittent puffs of white steam across the further view. And to the left, between the railway and the dark mass of the low hill beyond, dominating the whole view, colossal, inky-black, and crowned with smoke and fitful flames, stood the great cylinders of the Jeddah Company

Blast Furnaces, the central edifices of the big ironworks of which Horrocks was the manager. They stood heavy and threatening, full of an incessant turmoil of flames and seething molten iron, and about the feet of them rattled the rolling-mills, and the steam hammer beat heavily and splashed the white iron sparks hither and thither. Even as they looked, a truckful of fuel was shot into one of the giants, and the red flames gleamed out, and a confusion of smoke and black dust came boiling upwards towards the sky.

"Certainly you get some fine effects of colour with your furnaces," said Raut, breaking a silence that had become apprehensive.

Horrocks grunted. He stood with his hands in his pockets, frowning down at the dim steaming railway and the busy ironworks beyond, frowning as if he were thinking out some knotty problem.

Raut glanced at him and away again. "At present your moonlight effect is hardly ripe," he continued, looking upward. "The moon is still smothered by the vestiges of daylight."

Horrocks stared at him with the expression of a man who has suddenly awakened. "Vestiges of daylight? . . . . Of course, of course." He too looked up at the moon, pale still in the midsummer sky. "Come along," he said suddenly, and, gripping Raut's arm in his hand, made a move towards the path that dropped from them to the railway.

Raut hung back. Their eyes met and saw a thousand things in a moment that their eyes came near to say. Horrocks' hand tightened and then relaxed. He let go, and before Raut was aware of it, they were arm in arm, and walking, one unwillingly enough, down the path.

"You see the fine effect of the railway signals towards Burslem," said Horrocks, suddenly breaking into loquacity, striding fast, and tightening the grip of his elbow the while. " Little green lights and red and white lights, all against the haze. You have an eye for effect, Raut. It's a fine effect. And look at those furnaces of mine, how they rise upon us as we come down the hill. That to the right is my pet--seventy feet of him. I packed him myself, and he's boiled away cheerfully with iron in his guts for five long years. I've a particular fancy for HIM. That line of red there--a lovely bit of warm orange you'd call it, Raut--that's the puddlers' furnaces, and there, in the hot light, three black figures--did you see the white splash of the steam-hammer then?--that's the rolling mills. Come along! Clang, clatter, how it goes rattling across the floor! Sheet tin, Raut, --amazing stuff. Glass mirrors are not in it when that stuff comes from the mill. And, squelch!--there goes the hammer again. Come along!"

He had to stop talking to catch at his breath. His arm twisted into Raut's with benumbing tightness. He had come striding down the black path towards the railway as though he was possessed.

Raut had not spoken a word, had simply hung back against Horrocks' pull with all his strength.

"I say," he said now, laughing nervously, but with an undernote of snarl in his voice, "why on earth are you nipping my arm off, Horrocks, and dragging me along like this?"

At length Horrocks released him. His manner changed again. "Nipping your arm off?" he said. "Sorry. But it's you taught me the trick of walking in that friendly way."

"You haven't learnt the refinements of it yet then," said Raut, laughing artificially again. "By Jove! I'm black and blue."

Horrocks offered no apology. They stood now near the bottom of the hill, close to the fence that bordered the railway. The ironworks had grown larger and spread out with their approach. They looked up to the blast furnaces now instead of down; the further view of Etruria and Hanley had dropped out of sight with their descent. Before them, by the stile rose a notice-board, bearing still dimly visible, the words, "BEWARE OF THE TRAINS," half hidden by splashes of coaly mud.

"Fine effects," said Horrocks, waving his arm. "Here comes a train. The puffs of smoke, the orange glare, the round eye of light in front of it, the melodious rattle. Fine effects! But these furnaces of mine used to be finer, before we shoved cones in their throats, and saved the gas."

"How?" said Raut. "Cones?"

"Cones, my man, cones. I'll show you one nearer. The flames used to flare out of the open throats, great--what is it?--pillars of cloud by day, red and black smoke, and pillars of fire by night.

Now we run it off in pipes, and burn it to heat the blast, and the top is shut by a cone. You'll be interested in that cone."

"But every now and then," said Raut, "you get a burst of fire and smoke up there."

"The cone's not fixed, it's hung by a chain from a lever, and balanced by an equipoise. You shall see it nearer. Else, of course, there'd be no way of getting fuel into the thing. Every now and then the cone dips, and out comes the flare."

"I see," said Raut. He looked over his shoulder. "The moon gets brighter," he said.

"Come along," said Horrocks abruptly, gripping his shoulder again, and moving him suddenly towards the railway crossing. And then came one of those swift incidents, vivid, but so rapid that they leave one doubtful and reeling. Halfway across, Horrocks' hand suddenly clenched upon him like a vice, and swung him backward and through a half-turn, so that he looked up the line. And there a chain of lamp-lit carriage-windows telescoped swiftly as it came towards them, and the red and yellow lights of an engine grew larger and larger, rushing down upon them. As he grasped what this meant, he turned his face to Horrocks, and pushed with all his strength against the arm that held him back between the rails. The struggle did not last a moment. Just as certain as it was that Horrocks held him there, so certain was it that he had been violently lugged out of danger.

"Out of the way," said Horrocks, with a gasp, as the train came rattling by, and they stood panting by the gate into the ironworks.

"I did not see it coming," said Raut, still, even in spite of his own apprehensions, trying to keep up an appearance of ordinary intercourse.

Horrocks answered with a grunt. "The cone," he said, and then, as one who recovers himself, "I thought you did not hear."

"I didn't," said Raut.

"I wouldn't have had you run over then for the world," said Horrocks.

"For a moment I lost my nerve," said Raut.

Horrocks stood for half a minute, then turned abruptly towards the ironworks again. "See how fine these great mounds of mine, these clinker-heaps, look in the night! That truck yonder, up above there! Up it goes, and out-tilts the slag. See the palpitating red stuff go sliding down the slope. As we get nearer, the heap rises up and cuts the blast furnaces. See the quiver up above the big one. Not that way! This way, between the heaps. That goes to the puddling furnaces, but I want to show you the canal first." He came and took Raut by the elbow, and so they went along side by side. Raut answered Horrocks vaguely. What, he asked himself, had really happened on the line? Was he deluding himself with his own fancies, or had Horrocks actually held him back in the way of the train? Had he just been within an ace of being murdered?

Suppose this slouching, scowling monster DID know anything? For a minute or two then Raut was really afraid for his life, but the mood passed as he reasoned with himself. After all, Horrocks might have heard nothing. At any rate, he had pulled him out of the way in time. His odd manner might be due to the mere vague jealousy he had shown once before. He was talking now of the ash-heaps and the canal. "Eigh?" said Horrocks.

"What?" said Raut. "Rather! The haze in the moonlight. Fine!"

"Our canal," said Horrocks, stopping suddenly. "Our canal by moonlight and firelight is an immense effect. You've never seen it? Fancy that! You've spent too many of your evenings philandering up in Newcastle there. I tell you, for real florid effects-- But you shall see. Boiling water . . . "

As they came out of the labyrinth of clinker-heaps and mounds of coal and ore, the noises of the rolling-mill sprang upon them suddenly, loud, near, and distinct. Three shadowy workmen went by and touched their caps to Horrocks. Their faces were vague in the darkness. Raut felt a futile impulse to address them, and before he could frame his words, they passed into the shadows. Horrocks pointed to the canal close before them now: a weird-looking place it seemed, in the blood-red reflections of the furnaces. The hot water that cooled the tuyeres came into it, some fifty yards up-- a tumultuous, almost boiling affluent, and the steam rose up from the water in silent white wisps and streaks, wrapping damply about them, an incessant succession of ghosts coming up from the black and red eddies, a white uprising that made the head swim. The shining black tower of the larger blast-furnace rose overhead out of the mist, and its tumultuous riot filled their ears. Raut kept away from the edge of the water, and watched Horrocks.

"Here it is red," said Horrocks, "blood-red vapour as red and hot as sin; but yonder there, where the moonlight falls on it, and it drives across the clinker-heaps, it is as white as death."

Raut turned his head for a moment, and then came back hastily to his watch on Horrocks. "Come along to the rolling-mills," said Horrocks. The threatening hold was not so evident that time, and Raut felt a little reassured. But all the same, what on earth did Horrocks mean about "white as death" and "red as sin?" Coincidence, perhaps?

They went and stood behind the puddlers for a little while, and then through the rolling-mills, where amidst an incessant din the deliberate steam-hammer beat the juice out of the succulent iron, and black, half-naked Titans rushed the plastic bars, like hot sealing-wax, between the wheels. "Come on," said Horrocks in Raut's ear, and they went and peeped through the little glass hole behind the tuyeres, and saw the tumbled fire writhing in the pit of the blast-furnace. It left one eye blinded for a while. Then, with green and blue patches dancing across the dark, they went to the lift by which the trucks of ore and fuel and lime were raised to the top of the big cylinder.

And out upon the narrow rail that overhung the furnace, Raut's doubts came upon him again. Was it wise to be here? If Horrocks did know--everything! Do what he would, he could not resist a violent trembling. Right under foot was a sheer depth of seventy feet. It was a dangerous place. They pushed by a truck of fuel to get to the railing that crowned the place. The reek of the furnace, a sulphurous vapor streaked with pungent bitterness, seemed to make the distant hillside of Hanley quiver. The moon was riding out now from among a drift of clouds, halfway up the sky above the undulating wooded outlines of Newcastle. The steaming canal ran away from below them under an indistinct bridge, and vanished into the dim haze of the flat fields towards Burslem.

"That's the cone I've been telling you of," shouted Horrocks; "and, below that, sixty feet of fire and molten metal, with the air of the blast frothing through it like gas in soda-water."

Raut gripped the hand-rail tightly, and stared down at the cone. The heat was intense. The boiling of the iron and the tumult of the blast made a thunderous accompaniment to Horrocks' voice. But the thing had to be gone through now. Perhaps, after all . . .

"In the middle," bawled Horrocks, "temperature near a thousand degrees. If YOU were dropped into it . . . . flash into flame like a pinch of gunpowder in a candle. Put your hand out and feel the heat of his breath. Why, even up here I've seen the rain-water boiling off the trucks. And that cone there. It's a damned sight too hot for roasting cakes. The top side of it's three hundred degrees."

"Three hundred degrees!" said Raut.

"Three hundred centigrade, mind!" said Horrocks. "It will boil the blood out of you in no time."

"Eigh?" said Raut, and turned.

"Boil the blood out of you in . . . No, you don't!"

"Let me go!" screamed Raut. "Let go my arm!"

With one hand he clutched at the hand-rail, then with both. For a moment the two men stood swaying. Then suddenly, with a violent jerk, Horrocks had twisted him from his hold. He clutched at Horrocks and missed, his foot went back into empty air; in mid-air he twisted himself, and then cheek and shoulder and knee struck the hot cone together.

He clutched the chain by which the cone hung, and the thing sank an infinitesimal amount as he struck it. A circle of glowing red appeared about him, and a tongue of flame, released from the chaos within, flickered up towards him. An intense pain assailed him at the knees, and he could smell the singeing of his hands. He raised himself to his feet, and tried to climb up the chain, and then something struck his head. Black and shining with the moonlight, the throat of the furnace rose about him.

Horrocks, he saw, stood above him by one of the trucks of fuel on the rail. The gesticulating figure was bright and white in the moonlight, and shouting, "Fizzle, you fool! Fizzle, you hunter of women! You hot-blooded hound! Boil! boil! boil!"

Suddenly he caught up a handful of coal out of the truck, and flung it deliberately, lump after lump, at Raut.

"Horrocks!" cried Raut. "Horrocks!"

He clung crying to the chain, pulling himself up from the burning of the cone. Each missile Horrocks flung hit him. His clothes charred and glowed, and as he struggled the cone dropped, and a rush of hot suffocating gas whooped out and burned round him in a swift breath of flame.

His human likeness departed from him. When the momentary red had passed, Horrocks saw a charred, blackened figure, its head streaked with blood, still clutching and fumbling with the chain, and writhing in agony--a cindery animal, an inhuman, monstrous creature that began a sobbing intermittent shriek.

Abruptly, at the sight, the ironmaster's anger passed. A deadly sickness came upon him. The heavy odour of burning flesh came drifting up to his nostrils. His sanity returned to him.

"God have mercy upon me!" he cried. "O God! what have I done?"

He knew the thing below him, save that it still moved and felt, was already a dead man--that the blood of the poor wretch must be boiling in his veins. An intense realisation of that agony came to his mind, and overcame every other feeling. For a moment he stood irresolute, and then, turning to the truck, he hastily tilted its contents upon the struggling thing that had once been a man. The mass fell with a thud, and went radiating over the cone. With the thud the shriek ended, and a boiling confusion of smoke, dust, and flame came rushing up towards him. As it passed, he saw the cone clear again.

Then he staggered back, and stood trembling, clinging to the rail with both hands. His lips moved, but no words came to them.

Down below was the sound of voices and running steps. The clangour of rolling in the shed ceased abruptly.

A MOONLIGHT FABLE.

There was once a little man whose mother made him a beautiful suit of clothes. It was green and gold and woven so that I cannot describe how delicate and fine it was, and there was a tie of orange fluffiness that tied up under his chin. And the buttons in their newness shone like stars. He was proud and pleased by his suit beyond measure, and stood before the long looking-glass when first he put it on, so astonished and delighted with it that he could hardly turn himself away.

He wanted to wear it everywhere and show it to all sorts of people. He thought over all the places he had ever visited and all the scenes he had ever heard described, and tried to imagine what the feel of it would be if he were to go now to those scenes and places wearing his shining suit, and he wanted to go out forthwith into the long grass and the hot sunshine of the meadow wearing it. Just to wear it! But his mother told him, "No." She told him he must take great care of his suit, for never would he have another nearly so fine; he must save it and save it and only wear it on rare and great occasions. It was his wedding suit, she said. And she took his buttons and twisted them up with tissue paper for fear their bright newness should be tarnished, and she tacked little guards over the cuffs and elbows and wherever the suit was most likely to come to harm. He hated and resisted these things, but what could he do? And at last her warnings and persuasions had effect and he consented to take off his beautiful suit and fold it into its proper creases and put it away. It was almost as though he gave it up again. But he was always thinking of wearing it and of the supreme occasion when some day it might be worn without the guards, without the tissue paper on the buttons, utterly and delightfully, never caring, beautiful beyond measure.

One night when he was dreaming of it, after his habit, he dreamed he took the tissue paper from one of the buttons and found its brightness a little faded, and that distressed him mightily in his dream. He polished the poor faded button and polished it, and if anything it grew duller. He woke up and lay awake thinking of the brightness a little dulled and wondering how he would feel if perhaps when the great occasion (whatever it might be) should arrive, one button should chance to be ever so little short of its first glittering freshness, and for days and days that thought remained with him, distressingly. And when next his mother let him wear his suit, he was tempted and nearly gave way to the temptation just to fumble off one little bit of tissue paper and see if indeed the buttons were keeping as bright as ever.

He went trimly along on his way to church full of this wild desire. For you must know his mother did, with repeated and careful warnings, let him wear his suit at times, on Sundays, for example, to and fro from church, when there was no threatening of rain, no dust nor anything to injure it, with its buttons covered and its protections tacked upon it and a sunshade in his hand to shadow it if there seemed too strong a sunlight for its colours. And always, after such occasions, he brushed it over and folded it exquisitely as she had taught him, and put it away again.

Now all these restrictions his mother set to the wearing of his suit he obeyed, always he obeyed them, until one strange night he woke up and saw the moonlight shining outside his window. It seemed to him the moonlight was not common moonlight, nor the night a common night, and for a while he lay quite drowsily with this odd persuasion in his mind. Thought joined on to thought like things that whisper warmly in the shadows. Then he sat up in his little bed suddenly, very alert, with his heart beating very fast and a quiver in his body from top to toe. He had made up his mind. He knew now that he was going to wear his suit as it should be worn. He had no doubt in the matter. He was afraid, terribly afraid, but glad, glad.

He got out of his bed and stood a moment by the window looking at the moonshine-flooded garden and trembling at the thing he meant to do. The air was full of a minute clamor of crickets and murmurings, of the infinitesimal shouting of little living things. He went very gently across the creaking boards, for fear that he might wake the sleeping house, to the big dark clothes-press wherein his beautiful suit lay folded, and he took it out garment by garment and softly and very eagerly tore off its tissue-paper covering and its tacked protections, until there it was, perfect and delightful as he had seen it when first his mother had given it to him--a long time it seemed ago. Not a button had tarnished, not a thread had faded on this dear suit of his; he was glad enough for weeping as in a noiseless hurry he put it on. And then back he went, soft and quick, to the window and looked out upon the garden and stood there for a minute, shining in the moonlight, with his buttons twinkling like stars, before he got out on the sill and, making as little of a rustling as he could, clambered down to the garden path below. He stood before his mother's house, and it was white and nearly as plain as by day, with every window-blind but his own shut like an eye that sleeps. The trees cast still shadows like intricate black lace upon the wall.

The garden in the moonlight was very different from the garden by day; moonshine was tangled in the hedges and stretched in phantom cobwebs from spray to spray. Every flower was gleaming white or crimson black, and the air was aquiver with the thridding of small crickets and nightingales singing unseen in the depths of the trees.

There was no darkness in the world, but only warm, mysterious shadows; and all the leaves and spikes were edged and lined with iridescent jewels of dew. The night was warmer than any night had ever been, the heavens by some miracle at once vaster and nearer, and spite of the great ivory-tinted moon that ruled the world, the sky was full of stars.

The little man did not shout nor sing for all his infinite gladness. He stood for a time like one awe-stricken, and then, with a queer small cry and holding out his arms, he ran out as if he would embrace at once the whole warm round immensity of the world. He did not follow the neat set paths that cut the garden squarely, but thrust across the beds and through the wet, tall, scented herbs, through the night stock and the nicotine and the clusters of phantom white mallow flowers and through the thickets of southern-wood and lavender, and knee-deep across a wide space of mignonette. He came to the great hedge and he thrust his way through it, and though the thorns of the brambles scored him deeply and tore threads from his wonderful suit, and though burs and goosegrass and havers caught and clung to him, he did not care. He did not care, for he knew it was all part of the wearing for which he had longed. "I am glad I put on my suit," he said; "I am glad I wore my suit."

Beyond the hedge he came to the duck-pond, or at least to what was the duck-pond by day. But by night it was a great bowl of silver moonshine all noisy with singing frogs, of wonderful silver moonshine twisted and clotted with strange patternings, and the little man ran down into its waters between the thin black rushes, knee-deep and waist-deep and to his shoulders, smiting the water to black and shining wavelets with either hand, swaying and shivering wavelets, amid which the stars were netted in the tangled reflections of the brooding trees upon the bank. He waded until he swam, and so he crossed the pond and came out upon the other side, trailing, as it seemed to him, not duckweed, but very silver in long, clinging, dripping masses. And up he went through the transfigured tangles of the willow-herb and the uncut seeding grass of the farther bank. And so he came glad and breathless into the highroad. "I am glad," he said, "beyond measure, that I had clothes that fitted this occasion."

The highroad ran straight as an arrow flies, straight into the deep blue pit of sky beneath the moon, a white and shining road between the singing nightingales, and along it he went, running now and leaping, and now walking and rejoicing, in the clothes his mother had made for him with tireless, loving hands. The road was deep in dust, but that for him was only soft whiteness, and as he went a great dim moth came fluttering round his wet and shimmering and hastening figure. At first he did not heed the moth, and then he waved his hands at it and made a sort of dance with it as it circled round his head. "Soft moth!" he cried, "dear moth! And wonderful night, wonderful night of the world! Do you think my clothes are beautiful, dear moth? As beautiful as your scales and all this silver vesture of the earth and sky?"

And the moth circled closer and closer until at last its velvet wings just brushed his lips . . . . .

And next morning they found him dead with his neck broken in the bottom of the stone pit, with his beautiful clothes a little bloody and foul and stained with the duckweed from the pond. But his face was a face of such happiness that, had you seen it, you would have understood indeed how that he had died happy, never knowing the cool and streaming silver for the duckweed in the pond.

THE DIAMOND MAKER.

Some business had detained me in Chancery Lane nine in the evening, and thereafter, having some inkling of a headache, I was disinclined either for entertainment or further work. So much of the sky as the high cliffs of that narrow canon of traffic left visible spoke of a serene night, and I determined to make my way down to the Embankment, and rest my eyes and cool my head by watching the variegated lights upon the river. Beyond comparison the night is the best time for this place; a merciful darkness hides the dirt of the waters, and the lights of this transitional age, red glaring orange, gas-yellow, and electric white, are set in shadowy outlines of every possible shade between grey and deep purple. Through the arches of Waterloo Bridge a hundred points of light mark the sweep of the Embankment, and above its parapet rise the towers of Westminster,warm grey against the starlight. The black river goes by with only a rare ripple breaking its silence, and disturbing the reflections of the lights that swim upon its surface.

"A warm night," said a voice at my side.

I turned my head, and saw the profile of a man who was leaning over the parapet beside me. It was a refined face, not unhandsome, though pinched and pale enough, and the coat collar turned up and pinned round the throat marked his status in life as sharply as a uniform. I felt I was committed to the price of a bed and breakfast if I answered him.

I looked at him curiously. Would he have anything to tell me worth the money, or was he the common incapable--incapable even of telling his own story? There was a quality of intelligence in his forehead and eyes, and a certain tremulousness in his nether lip that decided me.

"Very warm," said I; "but not too warm for us here."

"No," he said, still looking across the water, "it is pleasant enough here . . . . just now."

"It is good," he continued after a pause, "to find anything so restful as this in London. After one has been fretting about business all day, about getting on, meeting obligations, and parrying dangers, I do not know what one would do if it were not for such pacific corners." He spoke with long pauses between the sentences. "You must know a little of the irksome labour of the world, or you would not be here. But I doubt if you can be so brain-weary and footsore as I am . . . . Bah! Sometimes I doubt if the game is worth the candle. I feel inclined to throw the whole thing over--name, wealth and position--and take to some modest trade. But I know if I abandoned my ambition--hardly as she uses me--I should have nothing but remorse left for the rest of my days."

He became silent. I looked at him in astonishment. If ever I saw a man hopelessly hard-up it was the man in front of me. He was ragged and he was dirty, unshaven and unkempt; he looked as though he had been left in a dust-bin for a week. And he was talking to ME of the irksome worries of a large business. I almost laughed outright. Either he was mad or playing a sorry jest on his own poverty.

"If high aims and high positions," said I, "have their drawbacks of hard work and anxiety, they have their compensations. Influence, the power of doing good, of assisting those weaker and poorer than ourselves; and there is even a certain gratification in display . . . . . "

My banter under the circumstances was in very vile taste. I spoke on the spur of the contrast of his appearance and speech. I was sorry even while I was speaking.

He turned a haggard but very composed face upon me. Said he: "I forgot myself. Of course you would not understand."

He measured me for a moment. "No doubt it is very absurd. You will not believe me even when I tell you, so that it is fairly safe to tell you. And it will be a comfort to tell someone. I really have a big business in hand, a very big business. But there are troubles just now. The fact is . . . . I make diamonds."

"I suppose," said I, "you are out of work just at present?"

"I am sick of being disbelieved," he said impatiently, and suddenly unbuttoning his wretched coat he pulled out a little canvas bag that was hanging by a cord round his neck. From this he produced a brown pebble. "I wonder if you know enough to know what that is?" He handed it to me.

Now, a year or so ago, I had occupied my leisure in taking a London science degree, so that I have a smattering of physics and mineralogy. The thing was not unlike an uncut diamond of the darker sort, though far too large, being almost as big as the top of my thumb. I took it, and saw it had the form of a regular octahedron, with the curved faces peculiar to the most precious of minerals. I took out my penknife and tried to scratch it--vainly. Leaning forward towards the gas-lamp, I tried the thing on my watch-glass, and scored a white line across that with the greatest ease.

I looked at my interlocutor with rising curiosity. "It certainly is rather like a diamond. But, if so, it is a Behemoth of diamonds. Where did you get it?"

"I tell you I made it," he said. "Give it back to me."

He replaced it hastily and buttoned his jacket. "I will sell it you for one hundred pounds," he suddenly whispered eagerly. With that my suspicions returned. The thing might, after all, be merely a lump of that almost equally hard substance, corundum, with an accidental resemblance in shape to the diamond. Or if it was a diamond, how came he by it, and why should he offer it at a hundred pounds?

We looked into one another's eyes. He seemed eager, but honestly eager. At that moment I believed it was a diamond he was trying to sell. Yet I am a poor man, a hundred pounds would leave a visible gap in my fortunes and no sane man would buy a diamond by gaslight from a ragged tramp on his personal warranty only. Still, a diamond that size conjured up a vision of many thousands of pounds. Then, thought I, such a stone could scarcely exist without being mentioned in every book on gems, and again I called to mind the stories of contraband and light-fingered Kaffirs at the Cape. I put the question of purchase on one side.

"How did you get it?" said I.

"I made it."

I had heard something of Moissan, but I knew his artificial diamonds were very small. I shook my head.

"You seem to know something of this kind of thing. I will tell you a little about myself. Perhaps then you may think better of the purchase." He turned round with his back to the river, and put his hands in his pockets. He sighed. "I know you will not believe me."

"Diamonds," he began--and as he spoke his voice lost its faint flavour of the tramp and assumed something of the easy tone of an educated man--are to be made by throwing carbon out of combination in a suitable flux and under a suitable pressure; the carbon crystallises out, not as black-lead or charcoal-powder, but as small diamonds. So much has been known to chemists for years, but no one yet had hit upon exactly the right flux in which to melt up the carbon, or exactly the right pressure for the best results. Consequently the diamonds made by chemists are small and dark, and worthless as jewels. Now I, you know, have given up my life to this problem--given my life to it.

"I began to work at the conditions of diamond making when I was seventeen, and now I am thirty-two. It seemed to me that it might take all the thought and energies of a man for ten years, or twenty years, but, even if it did, the game was still worth the candle. Suppose one to have at last just hit the right trick before the secret got out and diamonds became as common as coal, one might realize millions. Millions!"

He paused and looked for my sympathy. His eyes shone hungrily. "To think," said he, "that I am on the verge of it all, and here!

"I had," he proceeded, "about a thousand pounds when I was twenty-one, and this, I thought, eked out by a little teaching, would keep my researches going. A year or two was spent in study, at Berlin chiefly, and then I continued on my own account. The trouble was the secrecy. You see, if once I had let out what I was doing, other men might have been spurred on by my belief in the practicability of the idea; and I do not pretend to be such a genius as to have been sure of coming in first, in the case of a race for the discovery. And you see it was important that if I really meant to make a pile, people should not know it was an artificial process and capable of turning out diamonds by the ton. So I had to work all alone. At first I had a little laboratory, but as my resources began to run out I had to conduct my experiments in a wretched unfurnished room in Kentish Town, where I slept at last on a straw mattress on the floor among all my apparatus. The money simply flowed away. I grudged myself everything except scientific appliances. I tried to keep things going by a little teaching, but I am not a very good teacher, and I have no university degree, nor very much education except in chemistry, and I found I had to give a lot of time and labour for precious little money. But I got nearer and nearer the thing. Three years ago I settled the problem of the composition of the flux, and got near the pressure by putting this flux of mine and a certain carbon composition into a closed-up gun-barrel, filling up with water, sealing tightly, and heating."

He paused.

"Rather risky," said I.

"Yes. It burst, and smashed all my windows and a lot of my apparatus; but I got a kind of diamond powder nevertheless. Following out the problem of getting a big pressure upon the molten mixture from which the things were to crystallise, I hit upon some researches of Daubree's at the Paris Laboratorie des Poudres et Salpetres. He exploded dynamite in a tightly screwed steel cylinder, too strong to burst, and I found he could crush rocks into a muck not unlike the South African bed in which diamonds are found. It was a tremendous strain on my resources, but I got a steel cylinder made for my purpose after his pattern. I put in all my stuff and my explosives, built up a fire in my furnace, put the whole concern in, and--went out for a walk."

I could not help laughing at his matter-of-fact manner. "Did you not think it would blow up the house? Were there other people in the place?"

"It was in the interest of science," he said, ultimately. "There was a costermonger family on the floor below, a begging-letter writer in the room behind mine, and two flower-women were upstairs. Perhaps it was a bit thoughtless. But possibly some of them were out.

"When I came back the thing was just where I left it, among the white-hot coals. The explosive hadn't burst the case. And then I had a problem to face. You know time is an important element in crystallisation. If you hurry the process the crystals are small--it is only by prolonged standing that they grow to any size. I resolved to let this apparatus cool for two years, letting the temperature go down slowly during the time. And I was now quite out of money; and with a big fire and the rent of my room, as well as my hunger to satisfy, I had scarcely a penny in the world.

"I can hardly tell you all the shifts I was put to while I was making the diamonds. I have sold newspapers, held horses, opened cab-doors. For many weeks I addressed envelopes. I had a place as assistant to a man who owned a barrow, and used to call down one side of the road while he called down the other.

"Once for a week I had absolutely nothing to do, and I begged. What a week that was! One day the fire was going out and I had eaten nothing all day, and a little chap taking his girl out, gave me sixpence--to show off. Thank heaven for vanity! How the fish-shops smelt! But I went and spent it all on coals, and had the furnace bright red again, and then--Well, hunger makes a fool of a man.

"At last, three weeks ago, I let the fire out. I took my cylinder and unscrewed it while it was still so hot that it punished my hands, and I scraped out the crumbling lava-like mass with a chisel, and hammered it into a powder upon an iron plate. And I found three big diamonds and five small ones. As I sat on the floor hammering, my door opened, and my neighbour, the begging-letter writer came in. He was drunk--as he usually is. "'Nerchist,' said he. 'You're drunk,' said I. "Structive scoundrel,' said he. 'Go to your father,' said I, meaning the Father of Lies. 'Never you mind,' said he, and gave me a cunning wink, and hiccuped, and leaning up against the door, with his other eye against the door-post, began to babble of how he had been prying in my room, and how he had gone to the police that morning, and how they had taken down everything he had to say--"siffiwas a ge'm,' said he. Then I suddenly realised I was in a hole. Either I should have to tell these police my little secret, and get the whole thing blown upon, or be lagged as an Anarchist. So I went up to my neighbour and took him by the collar, and rolled him about a bit, and then I gathered up my diamonds and cleared out. The evening newspapers called my den the Kentish Town Bomb Factory. And now I cannot part with the things for love or money.

"If I go in to respectable jewellers they ask me to wait, and go and whisper to a clerk to fetch a policeman, and then I say I cannot wait. And I found out a receiver of stolen goods, and he simply stuck to the one I gave him and told me to prosecute if I wanted it back. I am going about now with several hundred thousand pounds-worth of diamonds round my neck, and without either food or shelter. You are the first person I have taken into my confidence. But I like your face and I am hard-driven."

He looked into my eyes.

"It would be madness," said I, "for me to buy a diamond under the circumstances. Besides, I do not carry hundreds of pounds about in my pocket. Yet I more than half believe your story. I will, if you like, do this: come to my office to-morrow . . . . "

"You think I am a thief!" said he keenly. "You will tell the police. I am not coming into a trap."

"Somehow I am assured you are no thief. Here is my card. Take that, anyhow. You need not come to any appointment. Come when you will."

He took the card, and an earnest of my good-will.

"Think better of it and come," said I.

He shook his head doubtfully. "I will pay back your half-crown with interest some day--such interest as will amaze you," said he. "Anyhow, you will keep the secret? . . . . Don't follow me."

He crossed the road and went into the darkness towards the little steps under the archway leading into Essex Street, and I let him go. And that was the last I ever saw of him.

Afterwards I had two letters from him asking me to send bank-notes--not cheques--to certain addresses. I weighed the matter over and took what I conceived to be the wisest course. Once he called upon me when I was out. My urchin described him as a very thin, dirty, and ragged man, with a dreadful cough. He left no message. That was the finish of him so far as my story goes. I wonder sometimes what has become of him. Was he an ingenious monomaniac, or a fraudulent dealer in pebbles, or has he really made diamonds as he asserted? The latter is just sufficiently credible to make me think at times that I have missed the most brilliant opportunity of my life. He may of course be dead, and his diamonds carelessly thrown aside--one, I repeat, was almost as big as my thumb. Or he may be still wandering about trying to sell the things. It is just possible he may yet emerge upon society, and, passing athwart my heavens in the serene altitude sacred to the wealthy and the well-advertised, reproach me silently for my want of enterprise. I sometimes think I might at least have risked five pounds.

THE LORD OF THE DYNAMOS.

The chief attendant of the three dynamos that buzzed and rattled at Camberwell, and kept the electric railway going, came out of Yorkshire, and his name was James Holroyd. He was a practical electrician, but fond of whisky, a heavy red-haired brute with irregular teeth. He doubted the existence of the deity, but accepted Carnot's cycle, and he had read Shakespeare and found him weak in chemistry. His helper came out of the mysterious East, and his name was Azuma-zi. But Holroyd called him Pooh-bah. Holroyd liked a nigger because he would stand kicking--a habit with Holroyd--and did not pry into the machinery and try to learn the ways of it. Certain odd possibilities of the negro mind brought into abrupt contact with the crown of our civilisation Holroyd never fully realised, though just at the end he got some inkling of them.

To define Azuma-zi was beyond ethnology. He was, perhaps, more negroid than anything else, though his hair was curly rather than frizzy, and his nose had a bridge. Moreover, his skin was brown rather than black, and the whites of his eyes were yellow. His broad cheekbones and narrow chin gave his face something of the viperine V. His head, too, was broad behind, and low and narrow at the forehead, as if his brain had been twisted round in the reverse way to a European's. He was short of stature and still shorter of English. In conversation he made numerous odd noises of no known marketable value, and his infrequent words were carved and wrought into heraldic grotesqueness. Holroyd tried to elucidate his religious beliefs, and--especially after whisky--lectured to him against superstition and missionaries. Azuma-zi, however, shirked the discussion of his gods, even though he was kicked for it.

Azuma-zi had come, clad in white but insufficient raiment, out of the stokehole of the Lord Clive, from the Straits Settlements, and beyond, into London. He had heard even in his youth of the greatness and riches of London, where all the women are white and fair, and even the beggars in the streets are white, and he arrived, with newly earned gold coins in his pocket, to worship at the shrine of civilisation. The day of his landing was a dismal one; the sky was dun, and a wind-worried drizzle filtered down to the greasy streets, but he plunged boldly into the delights of Shadwell, and was presently cast up, shattered in health, civilised in costume, penniless and, except in matters of the direst necessity, practically a dumb animal, to toil for James Holroyd and to be bullied by him in the dynamo shed at Camberwell. And to James Holroyd bullying was a labour of love.

There were three dynamos with their engines at Camberwell. The two that had been there since the beginning were small machines; the larger one was new. The smaller machines made a reasonable noise; their straps hummed over the drums, every now and then the brushes buzzed and fizzled, and the air churned steadily, whoo! whoo! whoo! between their poles. One was loose in its foundations and kept the shed vibrating. But the big dynamo drowned these little noises altogether with the sustained drone of its iron core, which somehow set part of the ironwork humming. The place made the visitor's head reel with the throb, throb, throb of the engines, the rotation of the big wheels, the spinning ball-valves, the occasional spittings of the steam, and over all the deep, unceasing, surging note of the big dynamo. This last noise was from an engineering point of view a defect, but Azuma-zi accounted it unto the monster for mightiness and pride.

If it were possible we would have the noises of that shed always about the reader as he reads, we would tell all our story to such an accompaniment. It was a steady stream of din, from which the ear picked out first one thread and then another; there was the intermittent snorting, panting, and seething of the steam engines, the suck and thud of their pistons, the dull beat on the air as the spokes of the great driving-wheels came round, a note the leather straps made as they ran tighter and looser, and a fretful tumult from the dynamos; and over all, sometimes inaudible, as the ear tired of it, and then creeping back upon the senses again, was this trombone note of the big machine. The floor never felt steady and quiet beneath one's feet, but quivered and jarred. It was a confusing, unsteady place, and enough to send anyone's thoughts jerking into odd zigzags. And for three months, while the big strike of the engineers was in progress, Holroyd, who was a blackleg, and Azuma-zi, who was a mere black, were never out of the stir and eddy of it, but slept and fed in the little wooden shanty between the shed and the gates.

Holroyd delivered a theological lecture on the text of his big machine soon after Azuma-zi came. He had to shout to be heard in the din. "Look at that," said Holroyd; "where's your 'eathen idol to match 'im?" And Azuma-zi looked. For a moment Holroyd was inaudible, and then Azuma-zi heard: "Kill a hundred men. Twelve per cent. on the ordinary shares," said Holroyd, "and that's something like a Gord!"

Holroyd was proud of his big dynamo, and expatiated upon its size and power to Azuma-zi until heaven knows what odd currents of thought that and the incessant whirling and shindy set up within the curly black cranium. He would explain in the most graphic manner the dozen or so ways in which a man might be killed by it, and once he gave Azuma-zi a shock as a sample of its quality. After that, in the breathing-times of his labour--it was heavy labour, being not only his own, but most of Holroyd's--Azuma-zi would sit and watch the big machine. Now and then the brushes would sparkle and spit blue flashes, at which Holroyd would swear, but all the rest was as smooth and rhythmic as breathing. The band ran shouting over the shaft, and ever behind one as one watched was the complacent thud of the piston. So it lived all day in this big airy shed, with him and Holroyd to wait upon it; not prisoned up and slaving to drive a ship as the other engines he knew--mere captive devils of the British Solomon--had been, but a machine enthroned. Those two smaller dynamos, Azuma-zi by force of contrast despised; the large one he privately christened the Lord of the Dynamos. They were fretful and irregular, but the big dynamo was steady. How great it was! How serene and easy in its working! Greater and calmer even than the Buddhas he had seen at Rangoon, and yet not motionless, but living! The great black coils spun, spun, spun, the rings ran round under the brushes, and the deep note of its coil steadied the whole. It affected Azuma-zi queerly.

Azuma-zi was not fond of labour. He would sit about and watch the Lord of the Dynamos while Holroyd went away to persuade the yard porter to get whisky, although his proper place was not in the dynamo shed but behind the engines, and, moreover, if Holroyd caught him skulking he got hit for it with a rod of stout copper wire. He would go and stand close to the colossus and look up at the great leather band running overhead. There was a black patch on the band that came round, and it pleased him somehow among all the clatter to watch this return again and again. Odd thoughts spun with the whirl of it. Scientific people tell us that savages give souls to rocks and trees--and a machine is a thousand times more alive than a rock or a tree. And Azuma-zi was practically a savage still; the veneer of civilisation lay no deeper than his slop suit, his bruises, and the coal grime on his face and hands. His father before him had worshipped a meteoric stone, kindred blood it may be had splashed the broad wheels of Juggernaut.

He took every opportunity Holroyd gave him of touching and hand, ling the great dynamo that was fascinating him. He polished and cleaned it until the metal parts were blinding in the sun. He felt a mysterious sense of service in doing this. He would go up to it and touch its spinning coils gently. The gods he had worshipped were all far away. The people in London hid their gods.

At last his dim feelings grew more distinct, and took shape in thoughts and at last in acts. When he came into the roaring shed one morning he salaamed to the Lord of the Dynamos, and then when Holroyd was away, he went and whispered to the thundering machine that he was its servant, and prayed it to have pity on him and save him from Holroyd. As he did so a rare gleam of light came in through the open archway of the throbbing machine-shed, and the Lord of the Dynamos, as he whirled and roared, was radiant with pale gold. Then Azuma-zi knew that his service was acceptable to his Lord. After that he did not feel so lonely as he had done, and he had indeed been very much alone in London. And even when his work time was over, which was rare, he loitered about the shed.

Then, the next time Holroyd maltreated him, Azuma-zi went presently to the Lord of the Dynamos and whispered, "Thou seest, O my Lord!" and the angry whir of the machinery seemed to answer him. Thereafter it appeared to him that whenever Holroyd came into the shed a different note came into the sounds of the dynamo. "My Lord bides his time," said Azuma-zi to himself. "The iniquity of the fool is not yet ripe." And he waited and watched for the day of reckoning. One day there was evidence of short circuiting, and Holroyd, making an unwary examination--it was in the afternoon--got a rather severe shock. Azuma-zi from behind the engine saw him jump off and curse at the peccant coil.

"He is warned," said Azuma-zi to himself. "Surely my Lord is very patient."

Holroyd had at first initiated his "nigger" into such elementary conceptions of the dynamo's working as would enable him to take temporary charge of the shed in his absence. But when he noticed the manner in which Azuma-zi hung about the monster he became suspicious. He dimly perceived his assistant was "up to something," and connecting him with the anointing of the coils with oil that had rotted the varnish in one place, he issued an edict, shouted above the confusion of the machinery, "Don't 'ee go nigh that big dynamo any more, Pooh-bah, or a'll take thy skin off!" Besides, if it pleased Azuma-zi to be near the big machine, it was plain sense and decency to keep him away from it.

Azuma-zi obeyed at the time, but later he was caught bowing before the Lord of the Dynamos. At which Holroyd twisted his arm and kicked him as he turned to go away. As Azuma-zi presently stood behind the engine and glared at the back of the hated Holroyd, the noises of the machinery took a new rhythm, and sounded like four words in his native tongue.

It is hard to say exactly what madness is. I fancy Azuma-zi was mad. The incessant din and whirl of the dynamo shed may have churned up his little store of knowledge and his big store of superstitious fancy, at last, into something akin to frenzy. At any rate, when the idea of making Holroyd a sacrifice to the Dynamo Fetich was thus suggested to him, it filled him with a strange tumult of exultant emotion.

That night the two men and their black shadows were alone in the shed together. The shed was lit with one big arc light that winked and flickered purple. The shadows lay black behind the dynamos, the ball governors of the engines whirled from light to darkness, and their pistons beat loud and steady. The world outside seen through the open end of the shed seemed incredibly dim and remote. It seemed absolutely silent, too, since the riot of the machinery drowned every external sound. Far away was the black fence of the yard with grey shadowy houses behind, and above was the deep blue sky and the pale little stars. Azuma-zi suddenly walked across the centre of the shed above which the leather bands were running, and went into the shadow by the big dynamo. Holroyd heard a click, and the spin of the armature changed.

"What are you dewin' with that switch?" he bawled in surprise. "Han't I told you--"

Then he saw the set expression of Azuma-zi's eyes as the Asiatic came out of the shadow towards him.

In another moment the two men were grappling fiercely in front of the great dynamo.

"You coffee-headed fool!" gasped Holroyd, with a brown hand at his throat. "Keep off those contact rings." In another moment he was tripped and reeling back upon the Lord of the Dynamos. He instinctively loosened his grip upon his antagonist to save himself from the machine.

The messenger, sent in furious haste from the station to find out what had happened in the dynamo shed, met Azuma-zi at the porter's lodge by the gate. Azuma-zi tried to explain something, but the messenger could make nothing of the black's incoherent English, and hurried on to the shed. The machines were all noisily at work, and nothing seemed to be disarranged. There was, however, a queer smell of singed hair. Then he saw an odd-looking crumpled mass clinging to the front of the big dynamo, and, approaching, recognised the distorted remains of Holroyd.

The man stared and hesitated a moment. Then he saw the face, and shut his eyes convulsively. He turned on his heel before he opened them, so that he should not see Holroyd again, and went out of the shed to get advice and help.

When Azuma-zi saw Holroyd die in the grip of the Great Dynamo he had been a little scared about the consequences of his act. Yet he felt strangely elated, and knew that the favour of the Lord Dynamo was upon him. His plan was already settled when he met the man coming from the station, and the scientific manager who speedily arrived on the scene jumped at the obvious conclusion of suicide. This expert scarcely noticed Azuma-zi, except to ask a few questions. Did he see Holroyd kill himself? Azuma-zi explained that he had been out of sight at the engine furnace until he heard a difference in the noise from the dynamo. It was not a difficult examination, being untinctured by suspicion.

The distorted remains of Holroyd, which the electrician removed from the machine, were hastily covered by the porter with a coffee-stained tablecloth. Somebody, by a happy inspiration, fetched a medical man. The expert was chiefly anxious to get the machine at work again, for seven or eight trains had stopped midway in the stuffy tunnels of the electric railway. Azuma-zi, answering or misunderstanding the questions of the people who had by authority or impudence come into the shed, was presently sent back to the stoke-hole by the scientific manager. Of course a crowd collected outside the gates of the yard--a crowd, for no known reason, always hovers for a day or two near the scene of a sudden death in London; two or three reporters percolated somehow into the engine-shed, and one even got to Azuma-zi; but the scientific expert cleared them out again, being himself an amateur journalist.

Presently the body was carried away, and public interest departed with it. Azuma-zi remained very quietly at his furnace, seeing over and over again in the coals a figure that wriggled violently and became still. An hour after the murder, to anyone coming into the shed it would have looked exactly as if nothing had ever happened there. Peeping presently from his engine-room the black saw the Lord Dynamo spin and whirl beside his little brothers, and the driving wheels were beating round, and the steam in the pistons went thud, thud, exactly as it had been earlier in the evening. After all, from the mechanical point of view, it had been a most insignificant incident--the mere temporary deflection of a current. But now the slender form and slender shadow of the scientific manager replaced the sturdy outline of Holroyd travelling up and down the lane of light upon the vibrating floor under the straps between the engines and the dynamos.

"Have I not served my Lord?" said Azuma-zi inaudibly, from his shadow, and the note of the great dynamo rang out full and clear. As he looked at the big whirling mechanism the strange fascination of it that had been a little in abeyance since Holroyd's death, resumed its sway.

Never had Azuma-zi seen a man killed so swiftly and pitilessly. The big humming machine had slain its victim without wavering for a second from its steady beating. It was indeed a mighty god.

The unconscious scientific manager stood with his back to him, scribbling on a piece of paper. His shadow lay at the foot of the monster.

"Was the Lord Dynamo still hungry? His servant was ready."

Azuma-zi made a stealthy step forward; then stopped. The scientific manager suddenly stopped writing, and walked down the shed to the endmost of the dynamos, and began to examine the brushes.

Azuma-zi hesitated, and then slipped across noiselessly into shadow by the switch. There he waited. Presently the manager's footsteps could be heard returning. He stopped in his old position, unconscious of the stoker crouching ten feet away from him. Then the big dynamo suddenly fizzled, and in another moment Azuma-zi had sprung out of the darkness upon him.

First, the scientific manager was gripped round the body and swung towards the big dynamo, then, kicking with his knee and forcing his antagonist's head down with his hands, he loosened the grip on his waist and swung round away from the machine. Then the black grasped him again, putting a curly head against his chest, and they swayed and panted as it seemed for an age or so. Then the scientific manager was impelled to catch a black ear in his teeth and bite furiously. The black yelled hideously.

They rolled over on the floor, and the black, who had apparently slipped from the vice of the teeth or parted with some ear--the scientific manager wondered which at the time--tried to throttle him. The scientific manager was making some ineffectual attempts to claw something with his hands and to kick, when the welcome sound of quick footsteps sounded on the floor. The next moment Azuma-zi had left him and darted towards the big dynamo. There was a splutter amid the roar.

The officer of the company who had entered, stood staring as Azuma-zi caught the naked terminals in his hands, gave one horrible convulsion, and then hung motionless from the machine, his face violently distorted.

"I'm jolly glad you came in when you did," said the scientific manager, still sitting on the floor.

He looked at the still quivering figure.

"It's not a nice death to die, apparently--but it is quick."

The official was still staring at the body. He was a man of slow apprehension.

There was a pause.

The scientific manager got up on his feet rather awkwardly. He ran his fingers along his collar thoughtfully, and moved his head to and fro several times.

"Poor Holroyd! I see now." Then almost mechanically he went towards the switch in the shadow and turned the current into the railway circuit again. As he did so the singed body loosened its grip upon the machine and fell forward on its face. The core of the dynamo roared out loud and clear, and the armature beat the air.

So ended prematurely the Worship of the Dynamo Deity, perhaps the most short-lived of all religions. Yet withal it could at least boast a Martyrdom and a Human Sacrifice.

THE COUNTRY OF THE BLIND.

Three hundred miles and more from Chimborazo, one hundred from the snows of Cotopaxi, in the wildest wastes of Ecuador's Andes, there lies that mysterious mountain valley, cut off from all the world of men, the Country of the Blind. Long years ago that valley lay so far open to the world that men might come at last through frightful gorges and over an icy pass into its equable meadows, and thither indeed men came, a family or so of Peruvian half-breeds fleeing from the lust and tyranny of an evil Spanish ruler. Then came the stupendous outbreak of Mindobamba, when it was night in Quito for seventeen days, and the water was boiling at Yaguachi and all the fish floating dying even as far as Guayaquil; everywhere along the Pacific slopes there were land-slips and swift thawings and sudden floods, and one whole side of the old Arauca crest slipped and came down in thunder, and cut off the Country of the Blind for ever from the exploring feet of men. But one of these early settlers had chanced to be on the hither side of the gorges when the world had so terribly shaken itself, and he perforce had to forget his wife and his child and all the friends and possessions he had left up there, and start life over again in the lower world. He started it again but ill, blindness overtook him, and he died of punishment in the mines; but the story he told begot a legend that lingers along the length of the Cordilleras of the Andes to this day.

He told of his reason for venturing back from that fastness, into which he had first been carried lashed to a llama, beside a vast bale of gear, when he was a child. The valley, he said, had in it all that the heart of man could desire--sweet water, pasture, an even climate, slopes of rich brown soil with tangles of a shrub that bore an excellent fruit, and on one side great hanging forests of pine that held the avalanches high. Far overhead, on three sides, vast cliffs of grey-green rock were capped by cliffs of ice; but the glacier stream came not to them, but flowed away by the farther slopes, and only now and then huge ice masses fell on the valley side. In this valley it neither rained nor snowed, but the abundant springs gave a rich green pasture, that irrigation would spread over all the valley space. The settlers did well indeed there. Their beasts did well and multiplied, and but one thing marred their happiness. Yet it was enough to mar it greatly. A strange disease had come upon them and had made all the children born to them there--and, indeed, several older children also--blind. It was to seek some charm or antidote against this plague of blindness that he had with fatigue and danger and difficulty returned down the gorge. In those days, in such cases, men did not think of germs and infections, but of sins, and it seemed to him that the reason of this affliction must he in the negligence of these priestless immigrants to set up a shrine so soon as they entered the valley. He wanted a shrine--a handsome, cheap, effectual shrine--to be erected in the valley; he wanted relics and such-like potent things of faith, blessed objects and mysterious medals and prayers. In his wallet he had a bar of native silver for which he would not account; he insisted there was none in the valley with something of the insistence of an inexpert liar. They had all clubbed their money and ornaments together, having little need for such treasure up there, he said, to buy them holy help against their ill. I figure this dim-eyed young mountaineer, sunburnt, gaunt, and anxious, hat brim clutched feverishly, a man all unused to the ways of the lower world, telling this story to some keen-eyed, attentive priest before the great convulsion; I can picture him presently seeking to return with pious and infallible remedies against that trouble, and the infinite dismay with which he must have faced the tumbled vastness where the gorge had once come out. But the rest of his story of mischances is lost to me, save that I know of his evil death after several years. Poor stray from that remoteness! The stream that had once made the gorge now bursts from the mouth of a rocky cave, and the legend his poor, ill-told story set going developed into the legend of a race of blind men somewhere "over there" one may still hear to-day.

And amidst the little population of that now isolated and forgotten valley the disease ran its course. The old became groping, the young saw but dimly, and the children that were born to them never saw at all. But life was very easy in that snow-rimmed basin, lost to all the world, with neither thorns nor briers, with no evil insects nor any beasts save the gentle breed of llamas they had lugged and thrust and followed up the beds of the shrunken rivers in the gorges up which they had come. The seeing had become purblind so gradually that they scarcely noticed their loss. They guided the sightless youngsters hither and thither until they knew the whole valley marvellously, and when at last sight died out among them the race lived on. They had even time to adapt themselves to the blind control of fire, which they made carefully in stoves of stone. They were a simple strain of people at the first, unlettered, only slightly touched with the Spanish civilisation, but with something of a tradition of the arts of old Peru and of its lost philosophy. Generation followed generation. They forgot many things; they devised many things. Their tradition of the greater world they came from became mythical in colour and uncertain. In all things save sight they were strong and able, and presently chance sent one who had an original mind and who could talk and persuade among them, and then afterwards another. These two passed, leaving their effects, and the little community grew in numbers and in understanding, and met and settled social and economic problems that arose. Generation followed generation. Generation followed generation. There came a time when a child was born who was fifteen generations from that ancestor who went out of the valley with a bar of silver to seek God's aid, and who never returned. Thereabout it chanced that a man came into this community from the outer world. And this is the story of that man.

He was a mountaineer from the country near Quito, a man who had been down to the sea and had seen the world, a reader of books in an original way, an acute and enterprising man, and he was taken on by a party of Englishmen who had come out to Ecuador to climb mountains, to replace one of their three Swiss guides who had fallen ill. He climbed here and he climbed there, and then came the attempt on Parascotopetl, the Matterhorn of the Andes, in which he was lost to the outer world.

The story of that accident has been written a dozen times. Pointer's narrative is the best. He tells how the little party worked their difficult and almost vertical way up to the very foot of the last and greatest precipice, and how they built a night shelter amidst the snow upon a little shelf of rock, and, with a touch of real dramatic power, how presently they found Nunez had gone from them. They shouted, and there was no reply; shouted and whistled, and for the rest of that night they slept no more.

As the morning broke they saw the traces of his fall. It seems impossible he could have uttered a sound. He had slipped eastward towards the unknown side of the mountain; far below he had struck a steep slope of snow, and ploughed his way down it in the midst of a snow avalanche. His track went straight to the edge of a frightful precipice, and beyond that everything was hidden. Far, far below, and hazy with distance, they could see trees rising out of a narrow, shut-in valley--the lost Country of the Blind. But they did not know it was the lost Country of the Blind, nor distinguish it in any way from any other narrow streak of upland valley. Unnerved by this disaster, they abandoned their attempt in the afternoon, and Pointer was called away to the war before he could make another attack. To this day Parascotopetl lifts an unconquered crest, and Pointer's shelter crumbles unvisited amidst the snows.

And the man who fell survived.

At the end of the slope he fell a thousand feet, and came down in the midst of a cloud of snow upon a snow-slope even steeper than the one above. Down this he was whirled, stunned and insensible, but without a bone broken in his body; and then at last came to gentler slopes, and at last rolled out and lay still, buried amidst a softening heap of the white masses that had accompanied and saved him. He came to himself with a dim fancy that he was ill in bed; then realized his position with a mountaineer's intelligence and worked himself loose and, after a rest or so, out until he saw the stars. He rested flat upon his chest for a space, wondering where he was and what had happened to him. He explored his limbs, and discovered that several of his buttons were gone and his coat turned over his head. His knife had gone from his pocket and his hat was lost, though he had tied it under his chin. He recalled that he had been looking for loose stones to raise his piece of the shelter wall. His ice-axe had disappeared.

He decided he must have fallen, and looked up to see, exaggerated by the ghastly light of the rising moon, the tremendous flight he had taken. For a while he lay, gazing blankly at the vast, pale cliff towering above, rising moment by moment out of a subsiding tide of darkness. Its phantasmal, mysterious beauty held him for a space, and then he was seized with a paroxysm of sobbing laughter . . . .

After a great interval of time he became aware that he was near the lower edge of the snow. Below, down what was now a moon-lit and practicable slope, he saw the dark and broken appearance of rock-strewn turf He struggled to his feet, aching in every joint and limb, got down painfully from the heaped loose snow about him, went downward until he was on the turf, and there dropped rather than lay beside a boulder, drank deep from the flask in his inner pocket, and instantly fell asleep . . . .

He was awakened by the singing of birds in the trees far below.

He sat up and perceived he was on a little alp at the foot of a vast precipice that sloped only a little in the gully down which he and his snow had come. Over against him another wall of rock reared itself against the sky. The gorge between these precipices ran east and west and was full of the morning sunlight, which lit to the westward the mass of fallen mountain that closed the descending gorge. Below him it seemed there was a precipice equally steep, but behind the snow in the gully he found a sort of chimney-cleft dripping with snow-water, down which a desperate man might venture. He found it easier than it seemed, and came at last to another desolate alp, and then after a rock climb of no particular difficulty, to a steep slope of trees. He took his bearings and turned his face up the gorge, for he saw it opened out above upon green meadows, among which he now glimpsed quite distinctly a cluster of stone huts of unfamiliar fashion. At times his progress was like clambering along the face of a wall, and after a time the rising sun ceased to strike along the gorge, the voices of the singing birds died away, and the air grew cold and dark about him. But the distant valley with its houses was all the brighter for that. He came presently to talus, and among the rocks he noted--for he was an observant man--an unfamiliar fern that seemed to clutch out of the crevices with intense green hands. He picked a frond or so and gnawed its stalk, and found it helpful.

About midday he came at last out of the throat of the gorge into the plain and the sunlight. He was stiff and weary; he sat down in the shadow of a rock, filled up his flask with water from a spring and drank it down, and remained for a time, resting before he went on to the houses.

They were very strange to his eyes, and indeed the whole aspect of that valley became, as he regarded it, queerer and more unfamiliar. The greater part of its surface was lush green meadow, starred with many beautiful flowers, irrigated with extraordinary care, and bearing evidence of systematic cropping piece by piece. High up and ringing the valley about was a wall, and what appeared to be a circumferential water channel, from which the little trickles of water that fed the meadow plants came, and on the higher slopes above this flocks of llamas cropped the scanty herbage. Sheds, apparently shelters or feeding-places for the llamas, stood against the boundary wall here and there. The irrigation streams ran together into a main channel down the centre of the valley, and this was enclosed on either side by a wall breast high. This gave a singularly urban quality to this secluded place, a quality that was greatly enhanced by the fact that a number of paths paved with black and white stones, and each with a curious little kerb at the side, ran hither and thither in an orderly manner. The houses of the central village were quite unlike the casual and higgledy-piggledy agglomeration of the mountain villages he knew; they stood in a continuous row on either side of a central street of astonishing cleanness, here and there their parti-coloured facade was pierced by a door, and not a solitary window broke their even frontage. They were parti-coloured with extraordinary irregularity, smeared with a sort of plaster that was sometimes grey, sometimes drab, sometimes slate-coloured or dark brown; and it was the sight of this wild plastering first brought the word "blind" into the thoughts of the explorer. "The good man who did that," he thought, "must have been as blind as a bat."

He descended a steep place, and so came to the wall and channel that ran about the valley, near where the latter spouted out its surplus contents into the deeps of the gorge in a thin and wavering thread of cascade. He could now see a number of men and women resting on piled heaps of grass, as if taking a siesta, in the remoter part of the meadow, and nearer the village a number of recumbent children, and then nearer at hand three men carrying pails on yokes along a little path that ran from the encircling wall towards the houses. These latter were clad in garments of llama cloth and boots and belts of leather, and they wore caps of cloth with back and ear flaps. They followed one another in single file, walking slowly and yawning as they walked, like men who have been up all night. There was something so reassuringly prosperous and respectable in their bearing that after a moment's hesitation Nunez stood forward as conspicuously as possible upon his rock, and gave vent to a mighty shout that echoed round the valley.

The three men stopped, and moved their heads as though they were looking about them. They turned their faces this way and that, and Nunez gesticulated with freedom. But they did not appear to see him for all his gestures, and after a time, directing themselves towards the mountains far away to the right, they shouted as if in answer. Nunez bawled again, and then once more, and as he gestured ineffectually the word "blind" came up to the top of his thoughts. "The fools must be blind," he said.

When at last, after much shouting and wrath, Nunez crossed the stream by a little bridge, came through a gate in the wall, and approached them, he was sure that they were blind. He was sure that this was the Country of the Blind of which the legends told. Conviction had sprung upon him, and a sense of great and rather enviable adventure. The three stood side by side, not looking at him, but with their ears directed towards him, judging him by his unfamiliar steps. They stood close together like men a little afraid, and he could see their eyelids closed and sunken, as though the very balls beneath had shrunk away. There was an expression near awe on their faces.

"A man," one said, in hardly recognisable Spanish. "A man it is--a man or a spirit--coming down from the rocks."

But Nunez advanced with the confident steps of a youth who enters upon life. All the old stories of the lost valley and the Country of the Blind had come back to his mind, and through his thoughts ran this old proverb, as if it were a refrain:--

"In the Country of the Blind the One-Eyed Man is King."

"In the Country of the Blind the One-Eyed Man is King."

And very civilly he gave them greeting. He talked to them and used his eyes.

"Where does he come from, brother Pedro?" asked one.

"Down out of the rocks."

"Over the mountains I come," said Nunez, "out of the country beyond there--where men can see. From near Bogota--where there are a hundred thousands of people, and where the city passes out of sight."

"Sight?" muttered Pedro. "Sight?"

"He comes," said the second blind man, "out of the rocks."

The cloth of their coats, Nunez saw was curious fashioned, each with a different sort of stitching.

They startled him by a simultaneous movement towards him, each with a hand outstretched. He stepped back from the advance of these spread fingers.

"Come hither," said the third blind man, following his motion and clutching him neatly.

And they held Nunez and felt him over, saying no word further until they had done so.

"Carefully," he cried, with a finger in his eye, and found they thought that organ, with its fluttering lids, a queer thing in him. They went over it again.

"A strange creature, Correa," said the one called Pedro. "Feel the coarseness of his hair. Like a llama's hair."

"Rough he is as the rocks that begot him," said Correa, investigating Nunez's unshaven chin with a soft and slightly moist hand. "Perhaps he will grow finer."

Nunez struggled a little under their examination, but they gripped him firm.

"Carefully," he said again.

"He speaks," said the third man. "Certainly he is a man."

"Ugh!" said Pedro, at the roughness of his coat.

"And you have come into the world?" asked Pedro.

"OUT of the world. Over mountains and glaciers; right over above there, half-way to the sun. Out of the great, big world that goes down, twelve days' journey to the sea."

They scarcely seemed to heed him. "Our fathers have told us men may be made by the forces of Nature," said Correa. "It is the warmth of things, and moisture, and rottenness--rottenness."

"Let us lead him to the elders," said Pedro.

"Shout first," said Correa, "lest the children be afraid. This is a marvellous occasion."

So they shouted, and Pedro went first and took Nunez by the hand to lead him to the houses.

He drew his hand away. "I can see," he said.

"See?" said Correa.

"Yes; see," said Nunez, turning towards him, and stumbled against Pedro's pail.

"His senses are still imperfect," said the third blind man. "He stumbles, and talks unmeaning words. Lead him by the hand."

"As you will," said Nunez, and was led along laughing.

It seemed they knew nothing of sight.

Well, all in good time he would teach them.

He heard people shouting, and saw a number of figures gathering together in the middle roadway of the village.

He found it tax his nerve and patience more than he had anticipated, that first encounter with the population of the Country of the Blind. The place seemed larger as he drew near to it, and the smeared plasterings queerer, and a crowd of children and men and women (the women and girls he was pleased to note had, some of them, quite sweet faces, for all that their eyes were shut and sunken) came about him, holding on to him, touching him with soft, sensitive hands, smelling at him, and listening at every word he spoke. Some of the maidens and children, however, kept aloof as if afraid, and indeed his voice seemed coarse and rude beside their softer notes. They mobbed him. His three guides kept close to him with an effect of proprietorship, and said again and again, "A wild man out of the rocks."

"Bogota," he said. "Bogota. Over the mountain crests."

"A wild man--using wild words," said Pedro. "Did you hear that--"BOGOTA? His mind has hardly formed yet. He has only the beginnings of speech."

A little boy nipped his hand. "Bogota!" he said mockingly.

"Aye! A city to your village. I come from the great world --where men have eyes and see."

"His name's Bogota," they said.

"He stumbled," said Correa--" stumbled twice as we came hither."

"Bring him in to the elders."

And they thrust him suddenly through a doorway into a room as black as pitch, save at the end there faintly glowed a fire. The crowd closed in behind him and shut out all but the faintest glimmer of day, and before he could arrest himself he had fallen headlong over the feet of a seated man. His arm, outflung, struck the face of someone else as he went down; he felt the soft impact of features and heard a cry of anger, and for a moment he struggled against a number of hands that clutched him. It was a one-sided fight. An inkling of the situation came to him and he lay quiet.

"I fell down," be said; I couldn't see in this pitchy darkness."

There was a pause as if the unseen persons about him tried to understand his words. Then the voice of Correa said: "He is but newly formed. He stumbles as he walks and mingles words that mean nothing with his speech."

Others also said things about him that he heard or understood imperfectly.

"May I sit up?" he asked, in a pause. "I will not struggle against you again."

They consulted and let him rise.

The voice of an older man began to question him, and Nunez found himself trying to explain the great world out of which he had fallen, and the sky and mountains and such-like marvels, to these elders who sat in darkness in the Country of the Blind. And they would believe and understand nothing whatever that he told them, a thing quite outside his expectation. They would not even understand many of his words. For fourteen generations these people had been blind and cut off from all the seeing world; the names for all the things of sight had faded and changed; the story of the outer world was faded and changed to a child's story; and they had ceased to concern themselves with anything beyond the rocky slopes above their circling wall. Blind men of genius had arisen among them and questioned the shreds of belief and tradition they had brought with them from their seeing days, and had dismissed all these things as idle fancies and replaced them with new and saner explanations. Much of their imagination had shrivelled with their eyes, and they had made for themselves new imaginations with their ever more sensitive ears and finger-tips. Slowly Nunez realised this: that his expectation of wonder and reverence at his origin and his gifts was not to be borne out; and after his poor attempt to explain sight to them had been set aside as the confused version of a new-made being describing the marvels of his incoherent sensations, he subsided, a little dashed, into listening to their instruction. And the eldest of the blind men explained to him life and philosophy and religion, how that the world (meaning their valley) had been first an empty hollow in the rocks, and then had come first inanimate things without the gift of touch, and llamas and a few other creatures that had little sense, and then men, and at last angels, whom one could hear singing and making fluttering sounds, but whom no one could touch at all, which puzzled Nunez greatly until he thought of the birds.

He went on to tell Nunez how this time had been divided into the warm and the cold, which are the blind equivalents of day and night, and how it was good to sleep in the warm and work during the cold, so that now, but for his advent, the whole town of the blind would have been asleep. He said Nunez must have been specially created to learn and serve the wisdom they had acquired, and that for all his mental incoherency and stumbling behaviour he must have courage and do his best to learn, and at that all the people in the door-way murmured encouragingly. He said the night--for the blind call their day night--was now far gone, and it behooved everyone to go back to sleep. He asked Nunez if he knew how to sleep, and Nunez said he did, but that before sleep he wanted food. They brought him food, llama's milk in a bowl and rough salted bread, and led him into a lonely place to eat out of their hearing, and afterwards to slumber until the chill of the mountain evening roused them to begin their day again. But Nunez slumbered not at all.

Instead, he sat up in the place where they had left him, resting his limbs and turning the unanticipated circumstances of his arrival over and over in his mind.

Every now and then he laughed, sometimes with amusement and sometimes with indignation.

"Unformed mind!" he said. "Got no senses yet! They little know they've been insulting their Heaven-sent King and master . . . . .

"I see I must bring them to reason.

"Let me think.

"Let me think."

He was still thinking when the sun set.

Nunez had an eye for all beautiful things, and it seemed to him that the glow upon the snow-fields and glaciers that rose about the valley on every side was the most beautiful thing he had ever seen. His eyes went from that inaccessible glory to the village and irrigated fields, fast sinking into the twilight, and suddenly a wave of emotion took him, and he thanked God from the bottom of his heart that the power of sight had been given him.

He heard a voice calling to him from out of the village.

"Yaho there, Bogota! Come hither!"

At that he stood up, smiling. He would show these people once and for all what sight would do for a man. They would seek him, but not find him.

"You move not, Bogota," said the voice.

He laughed noiselessly and made two stealthy steps aside from the path.

"Trample not on the grass, Bogota; that is not allowed."

Nunez had scarcely heard the sound he made himself. He stopped, amazed.

The owner of the voice came running up the piebald path towards him.

He stepped back into the pathway. "Here I am," he said.

"Why did you not come when I called you?" said the blind man. "Must you be led like a child? Cannot you hear the path as you walk?"

Nunez laughed. "I can see it," he said.

"There is no such word as SEE," said the blind man, after a pause. "Cease this folly and follow the sound of my feet."

Nunez followed, a little annoyed.

"My time will come," he said.

"You'll learn," the blind man answered. "There is much to learn in the world."

"Has no one told you, 'In the Country of the Blind the One-Eyed Man is King?'"

"What is blind?" asked the blind man, carelessly, over his shoulder.

Four days passed and the fifth found the King of the Blind still incognito, as a clumsy and useless stranger among his subjects.

It was, he found, much more difficult to proclaim himself than he had supposed, and in the meantime, while he meditated his coup d'etat, he did what he was told and learnt the manners and customs of the Country of the Blind. He found working and going about at night a particularly irksome thing, and he decided that that should be the first thing he would change.

They led a simple, laborious life, these people, with all the elements of virtue and happiness as these things can be understood by men. They toiled, but not oppressively; they had food and clothing sufficient for their needs; they had days and seasons of rest; they made much of music and singing, and there was love among them and little children. It was marvellous with what confidence and precision they went about their ordered world. Everything, you see, had been made to fit their needs; each of the radiating paths of the valley area had a constant angle to the others, and was distinguished by a special notch upon its kerbing; all obstacles and irregularities of path or meadow had long since been cleared away; all their methods and procedure arose naturally from their special needs. Their senses had become marvellously acute; they could hear and judge the slightest gesture of a man a dozen paces away--could hear the very beating of his heart. Intonation had long replaced expression with them, and touches gesture, and their work with hoe and spade and fork was as free and confident as garden work can be. Their sense of smell was extraordinarily fine; they could distinguish individual differences as readily as a dog can, and they went about the tending of llamas, who lived among the rocks above and came to the wall for food and shelter, with ease and confidence. It was only when at last Nunez sought to assert himself that he found how easy and confident their movements could be.

He rebelled only after he had tried persuasion.

He tried at first on several occasions to tell them of sight. "Look you here, you people," he said. "There are things you do not understand in me."

Once or twice one or two of them attended to him; they sat with faces downcast and ears turned intelligently towards him, and he did his best to tell them what it was to see. Among his hearers was a girl, with eyelids less red and sunken than the others, so that one could almost fancy she was hiding eyes, whom especially he hoped to persuade. He spoke of the beauties of sight, of watching the mountains, of the sky and the sunrise, and they heard him with amused incredulity that presently became condemnatory. They told him there were indeed no mountains at all, but that the end of the rocks where the llamas grazed was indeed the end of the world; thence sprang a cavernous roof of the universe, from which the dew and the avalanches fell; and when he maintained stoutly the world had neither end nor roof such as they supposed, they said his thoughts were wicked. So far as he could describe sky and clouds and stars to them it seemed to them a hideous void, a terrible blankness in the place of the smooth roof to things in which they believed--it was an article of faith with them that the cavern roof was exquisitely smooth to the touch. He saw that in some manner he shocked them, and gave up that aspect of the matter altogether, and tried to show them the practical value of sight. One morning he saw Pedro in the path called Seventeen and coming towards the central houses, but still too far off for hearing or scent, and he told them as much. "In a little while," he prophesied, "Pedro will be here." An old man remarked that Pedro had no business on path Seventeen, and then, as if in confirmation, that individual as he drew near turned and went transversely into path Ten, and so back with nimble paces towards the outer wall. They mocked Nunez when Pedro did not arrive, and afterwards, when he asked Pedro questions to clear his character, Pedro denied and outfaced him, and was afterwards hostile to him.

Then he induced them to let him go a long way up the sloping meadows towards the wall with one complaisant individual, and to him he promised to describe all that happened among the houses. He noted certain goings and comings, but the things that really seemed to signify to these people happened inside of or behind the windowless houses--the only things they took note of to test him by--and of those he could see or tell nothing; and it was after the failure of this attempt, and the ridicule they could not repress, that he resorted to force. He thought of seizing a spade and suddenly smiting one or two of them to earth, and so in fair combat showing the advantage of eyes. He went so far with that resolution as to seize his spade, and then he discovered a new thing about himself, and that was that it was impossible for him to hit a blind man in cold blood.

He hesitated, and found them all aware that he had snatched up the spade. They stood all alert, with their heads on one side, and bent ears towards him for what he would do next.

"Put that spade down," said one, and he felt a sort of helpless horror. He came near obedience.

Then he had thrust one backwards against a house wall, and fled past him and out of the village.

He went athwart one of their meadows, leaving a track of trampled grass behind his feet, and presently sat down by the side of one of their ways. He felt something of the buoyancy that comes to all men in the beginning of a fight, but more perplexity. He began to realise that you cannot even fight happily with creatures who stand upon a different mental basis to yourself. Far away he saw a number of men carrying spades and sticks come out of the street of houses and advance in a spreading line along the several paths towards him. They advanced slowly, speaking frequently to one another, and ever and again the whole cordon would halt and sniff the air and listen.

The first time they did this Nunez laughed. But afterwards he did not laugh.

One struck his trail in the meadow grass and came stooping and feeling his way along it.

For five minutes he watched the slow extension of the cordon, and then his vague disposition to do something forthwith became frantic. He stood up, went a pace or so towards the circumferential wall, turned, and went back a little way. There they all stood in a crescent, still and listening.

He also stood still, gripping his spade very tightly in both hands. Should he charge them?

The pulse in his ears ran into the rhythm of "In the Country of the Blind the One-Eyed Man is King."

Should he charge them?

He looked back at the high and unclimbable wall behind--unclimbable because of its smooth plastering, but withal pierced with many little doors and at the approaching line of seekers. Behind these others were now coming out of the street of houses.

Should he charge them?

"Bogota!" called one. "Bogota! where are you?"

He gripped his spade still tighter and advanced down the meadows towards the place of habitations, and directly he moved they converged upon him. "I'll hit them if they touch me," he swore; "by Heaven, I will. I'll hit." He called aloud, "Look here, I'm going to do what I like in this valley! Do you hear? I'm going to do what I like and go where I like."

They were moving in upon him quickly, groping, yet moving rapidly. It was like playing blind man's buff with everyone blindfolded except one. "Get hold of him!" cried one. He found himself in the arc of a loose curve of pursuers. He felt suddenly he must be active and resolute.

"You don't understand," he cried, in a voice that was meant to be great and resolute, and which broke. "You are blind and I can see. Leave me alone!"

"Bogota! Put down that spade and come off the grass!"

The last order, grotesque in its urban familiarity, produced a gust of anger. "I'll hurt you," he said, sobbing with emotion. "By Heaven, I'll hurt you! Leave me alone!"

He began to run--not knowing clearly where to run. He ran from the nearest blind man, because it was a horror to hit him. He stopped, and then made a dash to escape from their closing ranks. He made for where a gap was wide, and the men on either side, with a quick perception of the approach of his paces, rushed in on one another. He sprang forward, and then saw he must be caught, and SWISH! the spade had struck. He felt the soft thud of hand and arm, and the man was down with a yell of pain, and he was through.

Through! And then he was close to the street of houses again, and blind men, whirling spades and stakes, were running with a reasoned swiftness hither and thither.

He heard steps behind him just in time, and found a tall man rushing forward and swiping at the sound of him. He lost his nerve, hurled his spade a yard wide of this antagonist, and whirled about and fled, fairly yelling as he dodged another.

He was panic-stricken. He ran furiously to and fro, dodging when there was no need to dodge, and, in his anxiety to see on every side of him at once, stumbling. For a moment he was down and they heard his fall. Far away in the circumferential wall a little doorway looked like Heaven, and he set off in a wild rush for it. He did not even look round at his pursuers until it was gained, and he had stumbled across the bridge, clambered a little way among the rocks, to the surprise and dismay of a young llama, who went leaping out of sight, and lay down sobbing for breath.

And so his coup d'etat came to an end.

He stayed outside the wall of the valley of the blind for two nights and days without food or shelter, and meditated upon the Unexpected. During these meditations he repeated very frequently and always with a profounder note of derision the exploded proverb: "In the Country of the Blind the One-Eyed Man is King." He thought chiefly of ways of fighting and conquering these people, and it grew clear that for him no practicable way was possible. He had no weapons, and now it would be hard to get one.

The canker of civilisation had got to him even in Bogota, and he could not find it in himself to go down and assassinate a blind man. Of course, if he did that, he might then dictate terms on the threat of assassinating them all. But--Sooner or later he must sleep! . . . .

He tried also to find food among the pine trees, to be comfortable under pine boughs while the frost fell at night, and-- with less confidence--to catch a llama by artifice in order to try to kill it--perhaps by hammering it with a stone--and so finally, perhaps, to eat some of it. But the llamas had a doubt of him and regarded him with distrustful brown eyes and spat when he drew near. Fear came on him the second day and fits of shivering. Finally he crawled down to the wall of the Country of the Blind and tried to make his terms. He crawled along by the stream, shouting, until two blind men came out to the gate and talked to him.

"I was mad," he said. "But I was only newly made."

They said that was better.

He told them he was wiser now, and repented of all he had done.

Then he wept without intention, for he was very weak and ill now, and they took that as a favourable sign.

They asked him if he still thought he could SEE."

"No," he said. "That was folly. The word means nothing. Less than nothing!"

They asked him what was overhead.

"About ten times ten the height of a man there is a roof above the world--of rock--and very, very smooth. So smooth--so beautifully smooth . . "He burst again into hysterical tears. "Before you ask me any more, give me some food or I shall die!"

He expected dire punishments, but these blind people were capable of toleration. They regarded his rebellion as but one more proof of his general idiocy and inferiority, and after they had whipped him they appointed him to do the simplest and heaviest work they had for anyone to do, and he, seeing no other way of living, did submissively what he was told.

He was ill for some days and they nursed him kindly. That refined his submission. But they insisted on his lying in the dark, and that was a great misery. And blind philosophers came and talked to him of the wicked levity of his mind, and reproved him so impressively for his doubts about the lid of rock that covered their cosmic casserole that he almost doubted whether indeed he was not the victim of hallucination in not seeing it overhead.

So Nunez became a citizen of the Country of the Blind, and these people ceased to be a generalised people and became individualities to him, and familiar to him, while the world beyond the mountains became more and more remote and unreal. There was Yacob, his master, a kindly man when not annoyed; there was Pedro, Yacob's nephew; and there was Medina-sarote, who was the youngest daughter of Yacob. She was little esteemed in the world of the blind, because she had a clear-cut face and lacked that satisfying, glossy smoothness that is the blind man's ideal of feminine beauty, but Nunez thought her beautiful at first, and presently the most beautiful thing in the whole creation. Her closed eyelids were not sunken and red after the common way of the valley, but lay as though they might open again at any moment; and she had long eyelashes, which were considered a grave disfigurement. And her voice was weak and did not satisfy the acute hearing of the valley swains. So that she had no lover.

There came a time when Nunez thought that, could he win her, he would be resigned to live in the valley for all the rest of his days.

He watched her; he sought opportunities of doing her little services and presently he found that she observed him. Once at a rest-day gathering they sat side by side in the dim starlight, and the music was sweet. His hand came upon hers and he dared to clasp it. Then very tenderly she returned his pressure. And one day, as they were at their meal in the darkness, he felt her hand very softly seeking him, and as it chanced the fire leapt then, and he saw the tenderness of her face.

He sought to speak to her.

He went to her one day when she was sitting in the summer moonlight spinning. The light made her a thing of silver and mystery. He sat down at her feet and told her he loved her, and told her how beautiful she seemed to him. He had a lover's voice, he spoke with a tender reverence that came near to awe, and she had never before been touched by adoration. She made him no definite answer, but it was clear his words pleased her.

After that he talked to her whenever he could take an opportunity. The valley became the world for him, and the world beyond the mountains where men lived by day seemed no more than a fairy tale he would some day pour into her ears. Very tentatively and timidly he spoke to her of sight.

Sight seemed to her the most poetical of fancies, and she listened to his description of the stars and the mountains and her own sweet white-lit beauty as though it was a guilty indulgence. She did not believe, she could only half understand, but she was mysteriously delighted, and it seemed to him that she completely understood.

His love lost its awe and took courage. Presently he was for demanding her of Yacob and the elders in marriage, but she became fearful and delayed. And it was one of her elder sisters who first told Yacob that Medina-sarote and Nunez were in love.

There was from the first very great opposition to the marriage of Nunez and Medina-sarote; not so much because they valued her as because they held him as a being apart, an idiot, incompetent thing below the permissible level of a man. Her sisters opposed it bitterly as bringing discredit on them all; and old Yacob, though he had formed a sort of liking for his clumsy, obedient serf, shook his head and said the thing could not be. The young men were all angry at the idea of corrupting the race, and one went so far as to revile and strike Nunez. He struck back. Then for the first time he found an advantage in seeing, even by twilight, and after that fight was over no one was disposed to raise a hand against him. But they still found his marriage impossible.

Old Yacob had a tenderness for his last little daughter, and was grieved to have her weep upon his shoulder.

"You see, my dear, he's an idiot. He has delusions; he can't do anything right."

"I know," wept Medina-sarote. "But he's better than he was. He's getting better. And he's strong, dear father, and kind--stronger and kinder than any other man in the world. And he loves me--and, father, I love him."

Old Yacob was greatly distressed to find her inconsolable, and, besides--what made it more distressing--he liked Nunez for many things. So he went and sat in the windowless council-chamber with the other elders and watched the trend of the talk, and said, at the proper time, "He's better than he was. Very likely, some day, we shall find him as sane as ourselves."

Then afterwards one of the elders, who thought deeply, had an idea. He was a great doctor among these people, their medicine-man, and he had a very philosophical and inventive mind, and the idea of curing Nunez of his peculiarities appealed to him. One day when Yacob was present he returned to the topic of Nunez. "I have examined Nunez," he said, "and the case is clearer to me. I think very probably he might be cured."

"This is what I have always hoped," said old Yacob.

"His brain is affected," said the blind doctor.

The elders murmured assent.

"Now, WHAT affects it?"

"Ah!" said old Yacob.

THIS," said the doctor, answering his own question. "Those queer things that are called the eyes, and which exist to make an agreeable depression in the face, are diseased, in the case of Nunez, in such a way as to affect his brain. They are greatly distended, he has eyelashes, and his eyelids move, and consequently his brain is in a state of constant irritation and distraction."

"Yes?" said old Yacob. "Yes?"

"And I think I may say with reasonable certainty that, in order to cure him complete, all that we need to do is a simple and easy surgical operation--namely, to remove these irritant bodies."

"And then he will be sane?"

"Then he will be perfectly sane, and a quite admirable citizen."

"Thank Heaven for science!" said old Yacob, and went forth at once to tell Nunez of his happy hopes.

But Nunez's manner of receiving the good news struck him as being cold and disappointing.

"One might think," he said, "from the tone you take that you did not care for my daughter."

It was Medina-sarote who persuaded Nunez to face the blind surgeons.

"YOU do not want me," he said, "to lose my gift of sight?"

She shook her head.

"My world is sight."

Her head drooped lower.

"There are the beautiful things, the beautiful little things--the flowers, the lichens amidst the rocks, the light and softness on a piece of fur, the far sky with its drifting dawn of clouds, the sunsets and the stars. And there is YOU. For you alone it is good to have sight, to see your sweet, serene face, your kindly lips, your dear, beautiful hands folded together. . . . . It is these eyes of mine you won, these eyes that hold me to you, that these idiots seek. Instead, I must touch you, hear you, and never see you again. I must come under that roof of rock and stone and darkness, that horrible roof under which your imaginations stoop . . . NO; YOU would not have me do that?"

A disagreeable doubt had arisen in him. He stopped and left the thing a question.

"I wish," she said, "sometimes--" She paused.

"Yes?" he said, a little apprehensively.

"I wish sometimes--you would not talk like that."

"Like what?"

"I know it's pretty--it's your imagination. I love it, but NOW--"

He felt cold. "NOW?" he said, faintly.

She sat quite still.

"You mean--you think--I should be better, better perhaps--"

He was realising things very swiftly. He felt anger perhaps, anger at the dull course of fate, but also sympathy for her lack of understanding--a sympathy near akin to pity.

"DEAR," he said, and he could see by her whiteness how tensely her spirit pressed against the things she could not say. He put his arms about her, he kissed her ear, and they sat for a time in silence.

"If I were to consent to this?" he said at last, in a voice that was very gentle.

She flung her arms about him, weeping wildly. "Oh, if you would," she sobbed, "if only you would!"

For a week before the operation that was to raise him from his servitude and inferiority to the level of a blind citizen Nunez knew nothing of sleep, and all through the warm, sunlit hours, while the others slumbered happily, he sat brooding or wandered aimlessly, trying to bring his mind to bear on his dilemma. He had given his answer, he had given his consent, and still he was not sure. And at last work-time was over, the sun rose in splendour over the golden crests, and his last day of vision began for him. He had a few minutes with Medina-sarote before she went apart to sleep.

"To-morrow," he said, "I shall see no more."

"Dear heart!" she answered, and pressed his hands with all her strength.

"They will hurt you but little," she said; "and you are going through this pain, you are going through it, dear lover, for ME . . . . Dear, if a woman's heart and life can do it, I will repay you. My dearest one, my dearest with the tender voice, I will repay."

He was drenched in pity for himself and her.

He held her in his arms, and pressed his lips to hers and looked on her sweet face for the last time. "Good-bye!" he whispered to that dear sight, "good-bye!"

And then in silence he turned away from her.

She could hear his slow retreating footsteps, and something in the rhythm of them threw her into a passion of weeping.

He walked away.

He had fully meant to go to a lonely place where the meadows were beautiful with white narcissus, and there remain until the hour of his sacrifice should come, but as he walked he lifted up his eyes and saw the morning, the morning like an angel in golden armour, marching down the steeps . . . .

It seemed to him that before this splendour he and this blind world in the valley, and his love and all, were no more than a pit of sin.

He did not turn aside as he had meant to do, but went on and passed through the wall of the circumference and out upon the rocks, and his eyes were always upon the sunlit ice and snow.

He saw their infinite beauty, and his imagination soared over them to the things beyond he was now to resign for ever!

He thought of that great free world that he was parted from, the world that was his own, and he had a vision of those further slopes, distance beyond distance, with Bogota, a place of multitudinous stirring beauty, a glory by day, a luminous mystery by night, a place of palaces and fountains and statues and white houses, lying beautifully in the middle distance. He thought how for a day or so one might come down through passes drawing ever nearer and nearer to its busy streets and ways. He thought of the river journey, day by day, from great Bogota to the still vaster world beyond, through towns and villages, forest and desert places, the rushing river day by day, until its banks receded, and the big steamers came splashing by and one had reached the sea--the limitless sea, with its thousand islands, its thousands of islands, and its ships seen dimly far away in their incessant journeyings round and about that greater world. And there, unpent by mountains, one saw the sky--the sky, not such a disc as one saw it here, but an arch of immeasurable blue, a deep of deeps in which the circling stars were floating . . . .

His eyes began to scrutinise the great curtain of the mountains with a keener inquiry.

For example; if one went so, up that gully and to that chimney there, then one might come out high among those stunted pines that ran round in a sort of shelf and rose still higher and higher as it passed above the gorge. And then? That talus might be managed. Thence perhaps a climb might be found to take him up to the precipice that came below the snow; and if that chimney failed, then another farther to the east might serve his purpose better. And then? Then one would be out upon the amber-lit snow there, and half-way up to the crest of those beautiful desolations. And suppose one had good fortune!

He glanced back at the village, then turned right round and regarded it with folded arms.

He thought of Medina-sarote, and she had become small and remote.

He turned again towards the mountain wall down which the day had come to him.

Then very circumspectly he began his climb.

When sunset came he was not longer climbing, but he was far and high. His clothes were torn, his limbs were bloodstained, he was bruised in many places, but he lay as if he were at his ease, and there was a smile on his face.

From where he rested the valley seemed as if it were in a pit and nearly a mile below. Already it was dim with haze and shadow, though the mountain summits around him were things of light and fire. The mountain summits around him were things of light and fire, and the little things in the rocks near at hand were drenched with light and beauty, a vein of green mineral piercing the grey, a flash of small crystal here and there, a minute, minutely-beautiful orange lichen close beside his face. There were deep, mysterious shadows in the gorge, blue deepening into purple, and purple into a luminous darkness, and overhead was the illimitable vastness of the sky. But he heeded these things no longer, but lay quite still there, smiling as if he were content now merely to have escaped from the valley of the Blind, in which he had thought to be King. And the glow of the sunset passed, and the night came, and still he lay there, under the cold, clear stars.

Printed in Great Britain
by Amazon

16992268R00061